Superior Book Publishing Company
Van Nuys, California

Destiny's Godchild

a novel of
intrigue and enchantment
in frankish gaul

diana m. johnson

Superior Book Publishing Company
P.O. Box 8312
Van Nuys, CA 91409

Library of Congress Cataloging-in-Publication Data
Johnson, Diana M.
Destiny's Godchild: a novel/Diana M. Johnson
p. cm.
1. Pepin of Landon, known as "the Old" and "the Vain", Mayor of the Palace 622-639–Fiction. 2. Clothar II, King of Neustria 584-613, King of all Franks 613-629–Fiction. 3. Dagobert I, King of Austrasia 623-639, King of all Franks 629-639–Fiction. 4. Sigibert III, King of Austrasia 632-656–Fiction. 5. Clovis II, King of Neustria and Burgundy 639-657–Fiction. 6. Arnulf, Bishop of Metz 610-626–Fiction.
ISBN 0-9661504-0-6

To my grandfather,

Kenneth Daingerfield Pyle,

who, in tracing our family tree back to Pepin de Vain,

planted the seed for this novel.

Acknowledgments

Destiny's Godchild is a work of fiction set against the backdrop of actual events in history. While many characters are real, the conversations and motivations are figments of my own imagination, as is the main character, Egar, and all of those who were not of the royal court.

Many people have helped in the writing of my novel. I would especially like to thank my husband, Bill, and my mother, Grace Ellerbrock, for countless hours spent in reading and discussing the work in progress. I am grateful for the help of Professor Jack Lopez, California State University Northridge, and my Monday morning writer's group.

My thanks to magicians John Drebinger and Mike Wong at the Magic Castle in Hollywood, and especially manager E.J. Thacker. Never has research been so much fun.

Without libraries none of this could have been written and so I must express gratefulness for open stacks at the Oviatt Library, CSUN.

In addition, my gratitude to Betty Freeman, founder of the San Fernando Valley Branch of the California Writers Club for her very generous counsel and advice.

Words cannot convey my appreciation for Howard Goldstein who did far more than design a breathtakingly dramatic cover design.

Finally, my thanks to Eve Carram of UCLA for reading Destiny's Godchild, her valuable suggestions, and for declaring the novel, "a good read," and "worthy of publication".

Author's Note

When I was a little girl, my grandfather traced our family tree all the way back to Charlemagne's ancestor, the very first Pepin, known in history as Pepin of Landen or Pepin the Vain. I have since been intrigued by this period in history, standing between the ancient world and the middle ages—after the fall of the Roman Empire, before the reign of Charlemagne.

I wondered, even as a child, how it came about that Pepin the Vain, among others, acquired the power necessary to allow Charlemagne to become the greatest of the medieval kings. Was it as unknowing as historians write or did they have a sense of the part they were to play in preparing the way for Charlemagne to achieve his own destiny?

Destiny's Godchild

Chapter One

June, 617 A.D.

"Leave, Master? Without you?"

Young Egar's future suddenly loomed as empty as the pre-dawn sky from which all stars had faded. "I thought I would stay here always. Become your assistant."

The master laid his hand lightly on Egar's shoulder. "Ah, lad, I have no need for an assistant. My life's dream has been accomplished. Your destiny awaits discovery."

The master seemed to Egar to be one with the eastern sky heralding a new summer's day. His long, unbelted robe was a most unusual color. The gray of smoke, when the breeze stirred, it became the pearlescence of the dawn sky itself.

"But, where will I go?"

"Where the gods that guide your life direct."

"What *is* my destiny?"

"That is for you to learn. It is *your* destiny after all." Thin wisps of the master's white hair moved in the slight breeze like the feathery down that drifts from spent dandelion blossoms. "You cannot discover it by sitting safely on a warm hillside. You must search for it. Once found, only you can decide to what extent you will allow it to be your guide. Truly followed, your life will change the course of Frankish history."

The old master gazed fondly at his charge. The lad still had several inches to grow in order to balance his body with the size of his feet and hands... and the length of his nose. His thick brown hair glistened with traces of red. His dark eyes sparkled. Ruddy cheeks hinted at handsomeness yet to come.

In his mind's eye the old man saw the small child who had scampered up the hill with no knowledge that he was born of the gods. Those gods led Egar to this spot, forsaking his own family in order to live here and be trained by the master who waited patiently for his arrival. And now, in what seemed the blink of an eye, it was time for Egar to leave.

"But, how will I recognize my destiny? How will it happen?" Egar followed the master into the spacious cave that was their home.

"It could come to you in any number of ways, a dream perhaps, or a vision. Or the sense of recognizing a person or place you know you have never seen before."

"But do I know enough? Have I learned everything?" Egar absentmindedly stuffed clothing into a bag. It made him dizzy to think about the enormity of the outside world into which he was being thrust.

"Enough for today, and perhaps even tomorrow." The old master's eyes twinkled. "But wherever you go, take time to learn a phrase or two in a foreign tongue, the curing capacity of an unknown herb, a new mathematical formula, the shape of a starry constellation."

"Should I not stay just a little longer?" Egar begged. "You could teach me more of what I need."

"That is not to be. One piece of advice—not that you'll take notice of it. While you are skilled in many things, the one thing you do not have, that I can not give you, is maturity. Experience alone can supply this want. In the meantime it is wise to hold your council. Be not a braggart."

"What do you mean?" asked Egar.

"Earn your keep with juggling, small feats of sleight of hand, a ballad, an epic poem or two. But keep to yourself the deeper magic and the gift of sight which will grow when it is needed. People rightly fear what they do not understand and to be more than a little different can be dangerous. Come now and choose what you would like to take."

The master led the way to a large wooden trunk. Egar peered over his shoulder. "Colored rings for juggling. Scarves. Powder for making smoke. Am I taking too much?"

"No. You may take it all. I have no need of it," the master answered.

Egar sat on his haunches on the floor. His hands were filled with paraphernalia for the tricks he loved to perform. Already he felt more than a little lonesome. "Will I return?"

"Perhaps. Far in the future. Certainly not soon."

"Will I see you?"

"In your mind's eye, and perhaps in a dream or the smoke and flame of a fire."

"Will I be safe?"

"To live is to be at risk. There are many kinds of danger and many kinds of pain. In your long life you will experience your share of both.

"Now pack your belongings. I have obtained a mule to carry what you need and a horse for you to ride. Though he's no stallion, he is a right enough palfrey. You are not so large as to need a bigger animal and it is wiser for a traveler to show but humble possessions."

"A horse of my own? Where is it? Can I see it? And a mule, too? How did you manage to get them?"

The master layed a bony finger on Egar's mouth. "You will find the animals tethered at the foot of the hill."

Egar stood by the horse and heavily laden mule, so excited his previous reluctance to leave was forgotten. "Where shall I go first? What direction should I take?"

The master gently touched Egar's brow. He closed his eyes and stood silently for a few moments. Egar curbed his own impatience and tried to still his racing heart.

"Follow river and winding road. Meet danger with courage and cunning. You need not, as yet, understand. Just do as you are told. Go in peace. May the gods watch over you and bring you safely to your destination."

The master turned and without a backward glance, disappeared into the cave.

Egar was torn, longing to follow him, to have everything remain as it had always been, while at the same time, looking expectantly to what lay ahead. A few moments later, when the master did not reappear, Egar began his journey.

At first it was more a lark than a grand adventure. In his imagination he was an intrepid explorer, the very first to set eyes on unknown lands. Then he made believe he led a band of soldiers fearlessly into battle, or even better, led them back from successful conquest, his pack mule heavily laden with plundered gold and jewels.

Egar pondered what his true destiny might hold in store and how his life might be so important in Frankish history as to change its course. He seriously doubted he was fated to be either an explorer or a soldier. And yet, how else could he accomplish anything of historic consequence?

A wave of sadness swept over him as he thought once more of the master. Living with him in their snug cave had been all that any young boy could wish. He had experienced security and constant wonder at all there was to learn.

As tears threatened, Egar resolutely turned his thoughts from what could no longer be.

The sun rose. Sweat trickled down his face. He squirmed, trying unsuccessfully to reach an itch in the middle of his back.

The track narrowed as it dipped into a forest. Huge tree trunks crowded close together, their overarching branches creating a shadowy green tunnel. Egar breathed deeply of leafy-scented air.

Without warning, a band of rough-looking men appeared out of nowhere! Egar's heart pounded. Nowhere to run. Too late to hide.

The horse shied as a giant of a man grabbed its reins.

A tall, younger one swept Egar to the ground. In one motion he twisted Egar's arm behind his back. The other hand clamped over his mouth. Egar choked. Gagged on the stench of sweat and onions. Tears sprang to his eyes.

"Want you his throat slit?" asked Egar's captor. "Or his neck broke?" The younger man shrugged, indifferent to the method of death.

"Be not so eager, Amalgar," growled the huge man, his bulbous nose marred by an open wound. "Mayhap he be worth sommat alive. Once dead, we be not changing it."

Jolting agony shot through Egar as Amalgar jerked the pinioned arm. Egar bit down hard and tasted dirt and blood.

"By the bull! Ye be paying for that!" The muscular man pulled his hand from Egar's face. Sucked the wound. Egar gasped sweet fresh air.

"Young, but Jupiter's balls, he be spunky!" The leader laughed. "Into the trees! Bind and hobble him.

In camp we be learning what treasures we plundered."
He pulled Egar's horse into the forest.

A skinny little man grabbed the mule's rope and
scurried after him.

Where did *he* come from? Egar wondered

Amalgar pulled Egar's arm even higher, forcing him
to enter the woods on tip-toe. Let me not trip over a
rock or root, Egar prayed, else my arm will surely snap.
And little *he* cares!

Chapter Two

Ages later, or so it seemed to Egar, they arrived at a camp. A log smoldered in the rock-rimmed pit.

Egar sank gratefully to his knees. Sweat streamed down his face and back. Bound arms had made balance precarious while the leather thong shortened his footsteps to a shuffle. A powerful urge to urinate distracted him. With arms bound behind, how could he direct the stream?

During the nightmarish journey Egar learned the leader's name was Hugo. He looked to be in his mid years, with dirty fly-away graying brown hair and short, bushy beard. His arms were thicker than most men's thighs. One swipe of a huge paw-like hand could have sent Egar crashing.

Guy, the man leading the mule, had not uttered a word. Egar doubted he could speak. He seemed ancient. Small and wiry. Somewhat bent with the years. Egar noticed Guy constantly maneuvered to keep something, preferably Hugo, between himself and Amalgar.

Egar's captor boasted he had already killed more men than he could count.

"Untie his hands," ordered Hugo.

Pin-pricks shot up and down Egar's arms as Amalgar loosened the bonds. With a sigh, Egar struggled to his feet and hobbled to the edge of the clearing.

Amalgar squatted on his haunches. Flat, nearly lifeless eyes kept watch as Egar relieved himself.

"What treasure be our young friend carrying on his journey?" Hugo rummaged inside the packs on Egar's mule. "Bah! These be naught but baby's toys! Worthless rubbish."

Egar watched with dismay as ham-like hands tossed aside objects for juggling.

"By the dog, what make you of this?" Hugo pulled the small travel harp from its protective bag. Egar winced as the harp was carelessly turned this way and that.

"A fish trap, methinks," offered Amalgar. "Or perhaps a rabbit snare."

Ignorant slobs, thought Egar, have never seen a harp.

"The wood frame be good. It make a nice flame to cook our dinner." Hugo tossed Egar's prize possession toward the fire.

"My harp!" Egar shrieked.

He lunged. The thong binding his feet snapped taught, slamming him flat on the ground. For an agonizing moment pain filled his chest. He gasped, unable to catch his breath.

Egar was afraid to look up, knowing his beloved harp was reduced to splinters. But to his amazement, Guy held it safely in his arms. The old man had moved with astounding speed to save the instrument from destruction.

Amalgar laughed. "God's death! You should have seen your face! Now I know how to make you squirm!"

Egar had just begun to breathe normally. Now his heart stopped. Showing concern was a fatal mistake.

"Burn the junk, kill the boy, take the animals and go," suggested Amalgar.

"Wait! This 'junk' is of value—if you have skill." Egar dared not look at Amalgar. "I make my living juggling and playing the harp."

He had yet to earn his keep. Up to now he merely entertained the few families who lived scattered about the hillside near his master's cave.

"Show me," barked Hugo.

"Yes. Prove yourself," challenged Amalgar with a malicious smile.

Guy sat, cradling Egar's harp in his lap. An expectant look transformed his gaunt face.

Egar's heart plummeted. His hands shook. "I cannot juggle with my feet fettered. I must move my body to catch the rings as they fly."

"He brags but can do nothing," scoffed Amalgar. "Let me kill him."

Egar struggled to his feet. He shuffled to pick up the brightly-colored rings. Concentrate, he told himself. Ignore the outlaws. Keep your eyes on the rings.

A yellow ring soared into the blue sky of the small clearing. It wobbled, but Egar caught it. The second flight was smoother. Soon a red one joined its cousin and then the green. From hand to hand and into the air.

So focused was Egar, the forest and its outlaws all but disappeared. He slid a blue ring down his arm, planning to send it spinning between the circling yellow one and the red. Change the pattern to two up and two down.

He took a step to re-position his body and—fell again as the hobble jerked him short.

Sick with frustration, Egar nearly retched. His one chance—gone.

"Jupiter's balls!" exclaimed Hugo. "He be telling the truth. He do be worth sommat, after all! Take him to market day—"

"—and I pass the basket for food and mayhap a coin or two—" interrupted Amalgar.

"—and I work the crowd. See what sticks to me fingers!" finished Guy.

He *does* speak, after all thought Egar.

Sleep was slow in coming that night. Egar lay on his side, hands and feet firmly bound. Night sounds were different under the shadowy shapes of towering trees—strange bird calls, scurrying nocturnal animals. So unlike the safe silence of the cave.

The master lied, Egar finally admitted to himself. I have no destiny. No gods direct my life. The master was but tired of my company. Prisoner of outlaws. Forever watching over my shoulder.

The future yawned like a malevolent pit.

After weeks of traveling, following feast days and local celebrations, Egar looked as much an outlaw as the rest. His everyday tunic was ragged and grimy. His good linen shirt and sleeveless mantle of brilliant green were kept carefully wrapped. Worn only for the performances which provided them with food.

Hugo's leather breeches were stiff with accumulated dirt, his tunic equally filthy. Old Guy wore no stockings. Dirty, scrawny legs disappeared into ill-fitting boots.

Only Amalgar looked presentable. Every night he wiped the mud and dust of travel from his soft leather boots. He took care where he sat in his coarse linen breeches. Dirt and grease seemed not to fly to the front of his short, fringed tunic of blue cloth, the way it did to the clothing of the others. He seemed pleasant enough—unless you looked into his cold, mocking eyes.

Egar was so busy dodging the drunken abuses of the outlaws and working to get enough to eat he had little chance to recall the Old Master's prediction of his impact on history. But being of a sharp and inquiring mind he did pick up much new learning—the sly ways of street urchins, coarse language not to be found in any book and how to engage the temper and support of constantly changing gatherings.

The band traveled westward, the hamlets gradually growing bigger, until they came to Amiens on the Somme River. The town was huge. Quite the largest Egar had ever seen. It was old, too. Or so Hugo said. Conquered by Caesar and later overrun by the Huns.

An air of festivity permeated the place. Flowers and streamers decorated most of the buildings—and all of the winsome maidens. A band of musicians added drum, tambourine and flute to the cacophony. The outlaws claimed a spot between an ale vendor and a seller of sweetmeats.

Guy carefully set on the ground the sack of juggling paraphernalia he'd been carrying. He looked for a moment at Amalgar talking to Hugo and gesturing to the other side of the open square. Guy turned and gave Egar a wink and a shy smile before slipping silently into the crowd.

Egar began juggling rings—first two to draw a crowd then, three and four. Out of the corner of his eye he saw a girl wearing a daisy crown. She smiled, white teeth flashing. Brown curls framed startlingly blue eyes and sun-blushed cheeks. Egar returned her smile. Rings fell, rolling in all directions. Children in the crowd scampered after them. Egar could feel his own cheeks heating. Knew they were turning crimson. The girl laughed, the sound sweeter than any bell Egar had ever heard.

Their eyes locked, sharing the secret that she was the cause of the fly-away rings. Egar caught Amalgar's cold stare and his laughter abruptly choked in his throat.

Egar began juggling again, centering his concentration until all seven colored rings were in the air. People cheered as the rings descended to his outstretched arm. Egar took an exaggerated bow and looked. The girl had disappeared.

Amalgar circulated the basket. Someone flipped in a penny but it skipped out again to roll on the ground near Egar's feet. He sprang after it.

Steeling himself, he engaged Amalgar's eyes. A duel. Who would look away first? Egar dropped the penny into the basket. They both heard its solid "clunk" against the other coins. He held Amalgar's stare a moment longer, then lowered his eyes. Amalgar chuckled with sinister glee. He'd won!

Egar turned and began gathering his paraphernalia. He dared not show his face. Amalgar might read triumph there instead of defeat. While dropping in the penny, Egar palmed a coin of greater value! He kept his skill at sleight-of-hand his own secret and put it to good use when he had the chance.

The vendors gave them food and ale in gratitude for drawing a crowd to their corner of the open-air market.

Hugo snored more deeply than usual. With a rustling of dry leaves, Guy turned in his sleep. But—and Egar well realized this was the second most momentous event of the day—Amalgar had not returned with them.

He was probably seducing the blue-eyed girl with the daisy crown. Egar hoped not, for the girl's sake.

Amalgar could be brutal. Once Egar had seen him pick up a cat by the tail and swing it, yowling and clawing the air, around and around over his head. After three or four spins he flung it at a wall and grunted with satisfaction as the animal hit and splattered—blood, guts and bits of fur clinging to the rough wood surface. No remorse. Even less reason.

Egar fervently hoped the laughing girl had gone off with some other young man.

Cautiously Egar moved his arms and legs under the blanket. Of the whole enchanted day, *this* was the most wondrous thing to happen. Hugo had drunk most of Egar's share of the free ale and Guy's as well.

By the time the three of them returned to camp, Hugo was bleary-eyed and singing lustily. They all tumbled onto their pallets of dried leaves and blankets.

Only—for the first time ever—Hugo *forgot to bind Egar's hands and feet!*

Egar sat up cautiously.

"Psssst."

He froze.

"Psssst!"

He turned. Moonlight glinted in Guy's open eyes. Egar's euphoria dissipated like smoke. His best ever chance to escape—gone.

Guy motioned for Egar to come closer. Curious, he did.

"Here. Take." Guy dropped one, two, three precious coins into Egar's hand. Business had been brisk for the pick-pocket as well. "I be saving 'em for ye. Now go whilst ye can!"

Chapter Three

Keeping his animals to the darkest shadows, Egar
crept back into Amiens. With the coins for his passage
clutched in his fist, he boarded a deep, bowl-shaped
trading ship. It set sail with the tide for the Narrow Sea
and Greater Britain. Egar grasped the rail in the
darkness. Everything was new and different—from the
tangy scent of marshlands and salt water to the queasy
sensations in his stomach created by the rolling
motion.

As the sky lightened in the east, the strip of
constantly-moving ocean grew wider—cutting his last
links with the master. Shafts of light danced off the
water and stabbed his eyes making his head ache.
Utterly alone, Egar sighed.

Once docked, he found an ale house where he
could earn his way. The air of the low-ceilinged public
room was redolent of wood smoke and warm bodies.

A man made room for Egar on the bench. "How be
ye called, stranger? And where be ye from?"

Before Egar could answer, a young girl set a large
trencher of mutton stew on the table. From her apron,
she brought two large loaves of crusty bread. The

loaves passed from hand to hand, each man cutting a thick slice with his hunting knife. The same knives speared chunks of meat and vegetables while the men dunked their bread into the trencher to sop up the savory juices.

"That be innkeeper's daughter," the friendly man informed Egar.

"Gisela, lass, how about some ale?" asked another. Immediately every man held out the mug he carried.

She returned, carrying the heavy mugs close. Her reddish-blond hair covered cheeks pink with exertion. As she put Egar's ale in front of him, he couldn't help but notice how her firm young breasts strained at the fabric of her bodice. When she turned her blue eyes to look at him, he saw curiosity there, and something more. Leaning over to pick up the empty trencher she brushed against Egar's shoulder, creating a ripple of excitement.

Afterwards Egar removed the covering from his travel harp. The men at the tables watched intently as he tuned the strings, then swept a chord across them.

The silence that followed was alive with expectation. Knives lay unheeded on plates. Mugs were held suspended between table and lips. Even Gisela paused in her trips between kitchen building and tables to listen. Keenly aware of her presence, Egar sat even straighter. Filled with a sense of power, he knew he had captured every eye and ear. He paused for one more long moment and then, like dropping a stone into a pool of calm water, broke the silence with his song.

The next morning Gisela stopped him at the door.

"Have you seen the standing stones?" she asked.

"No. What are they?"

"Wondrously huge stones which have stood on end since the beginning of time."

"Here?"

"Nearby. In Stonehenge."

* * *

The touch of her warm body riding behind him made Egar's head whirl. She held an arm around his waist. Her soft breasts pressed into his back. The usually articulate balladeer could think of nothing to say.

The horse followed the ancient Roman road. Although most of the paving stones had been taken, constant use made it easily followed. It led to a field of giant gray stones.

Egar and Gisela gazed at the great monoliths, many with lintels still forming arches. Here and there fallen stones lay like huge gray beasts in the grass and weeds. Filled with awe, Egar wondered how long they had stood thus. What ceremonies they had seen. To what gods they had been raised.

"What see you?" Gisela asked.

"There is something here," he responded in a breathless voice. "Even after all these countless years. I feel it, but know not what it is."

Egar walked around the outer circle of gigantic pillars, each more than twice a man's height. Reverently he touched their sides, feeling marks where ancient men had hewn them.

"Was it magic or design that put them thus?"

"Probably more than a little of each," Gisela responded.

They walked slowly hand in hand to the inner circle of somewhat smaller monoliths.

"This was a place of great learning," she whispered. "Countless years ago priests studied the sun, moon and stars here. It was their temple as well. They knew secrets of the universe now long lost."

"How do you know all this?" he asked.

Gisela's eyes widened and she looked around hastily. "I... I do not know. Perhaps I heard it while serving meals."

"Why are you frightened?"

"I... I am... I do not know what you mean."

Looking deep into her eyes, Egar held both of her hands in his. "I feel something special here. Perhaps I could learn about these stones and those who set them here. Take me to someone who knows of this, I beg you."

"I... I... don't..." she stammered. "I cannot help you."

"But you said there were priests who learned and worshipped here. I want to talk to the one who told you so."

Gisela drew away. "Be you Christian?"

"Why do you ask?"

"Be you one of St. Augustine's men, sent from the Pope in Rome to convert the pagans?"

He almost laughed. "No. I assure you."

"Would knowledge of pagan gods shock you?"

"No. I respect all gods, pagan and Christian alike."

"That could be dangerous to say."

Egar suddenly realized that in serving the ancient ones himself, he had forgotten how strongly Christians felt theirs was the only true faith. To what lengths they would go to protect their faith.

At the sudden comprehension in his eyes she said, "Not from me, mind you. I would do naught to hurt you. But guard your tongue."

Egar remembered his old master saying somewhat the same thing to him on more than one occasion.

"Be you a sorcerer?" She cocked her head to one side.

"What does a sorcerer do?"

"Destroys enemies, cures sickness, makes crops grow, women fruitful, rain fall—all by magic."

Egar pondered. "I have some gifts beyond mere sleight of hand, but I cannot do all *that*, so I must not be one. At least no one has ever called me such. Must I be, to learn the message of this place?"

"I cannot talk to you of the secrets of Stonehenge."

Egar willed the ancient stones to speak to him. But they remained silent.

He gazed in awe at five huge sarsen trilithons arranged in a horseshoe inside the inner circle. Each was at least four times the height of a man. Egar stepped inside, facing what he instinctively knew to be the altar stone. His skin prickled. He dared not approach it. He did not know enough.

They talked very little, content to sit close together at the foot of a monolith, sharing the meal they had brought. Egar's eyes turned again and again to Gisela. He was captivated by her creamy white, firmly plump body. Having shared his master's monastic life, he had never before been so close to a young maiden. He lifted a tentative finger to brush aside the golden hair from her forehead. She did not draw away.

Slowly he traced the curve of her cheek, the outline of her lips. She smiled, showing small white teeth. Breathlessly, his lips were drawn to hers. Ecstasy.

He peeled off her bodice and chemise to better feel the swelling of her breasts.

His erection strained at his breeches. She let loose the string holding them to his waist. He felt no shame that she should see his nude body. If the old gods watched, they did so without censure.

Perhaps they reached across the ages to take his hand because at that instant Egar felt himself being pulled in two. Part of him rose out of his body as if riding the wings of a hawk while the earthbound Egar fingered the tips of Gisela's breasts grown firm with his caress.

The soaring Egar looked down on the figures of himself and Gisela as if from a great height. The two young people grew smaller and smaller as he rose into the blue sky. The brooding stones stood guard over the lovers. Egar was there but not there, ensnared and yet detached. He wanted with all his heart to lose himself in Gisela's body but was also drawn into the sky. As the earth fell away, the stones made small by the distance, he saw the sun glint on the blue waters of the Narrow Sea. With the freedom of a bird he rode the air currents. He saw his homeland and in the distance, lands beyond his knowledge, seas beyond his experience.

Egar yearned to discover the wonders of the unknown to which this amazing flight had given him a tantalizing glimpse. Then as the earth-bound Egar entered Gisela with urgency that would not be denied, the soaring Egar was covered with a shower of sparks as of hundreds of falling stars. He plummeted.

Egar exploded with pent-up desire, fully occupying his own body once again. Arching her back, Gisela gave a cry of delight and welcomed him. Slowly at first and then with greater intensity they abandoned themselves to the age-old rhythms. Afterwards they lay, arms entwined, bodies together, panting for breath.

Egar wiped away a tear. "Why do you weep? Did I hurt you?"

"No. Nor would you ever, willingly," she responded. "But you will follow where the gods lead you. You will fly on falcon's wings and see what most men cannot even dream of."

"But how... how could you see the vision of my flight?" he stammered.

"Thy love was so great it took me with you."

Egar pondered what she said, but it was beyond his comprehension.

As they later rode back to the ale house, Gisela's warm body now familiar against his back, Egar wondered why his old master never told him how wonderful a female could be. Had he ever experienced the warmth of a woman? Egar felt a rush of compassion for the man who lived such a celibate life. He could not imagine what it would be like to live alone forever. It was a fate too awful to contemplate.

Chapter Four

Egar lived for the sight of Gisela. He was the first each morning to wash his face in the cold water of the trough, hopeful of seeing her as she went about her work. When serving at table, if she brushed her body against his, he glowed with a burning warmth at being touched.

Each time he saw her he felt a welling of excitement and knew his cheeks were flaming. He soon learned when he could expect to find her in the garden and willingly helped gather fresh vegetables. He wanted to be with her every moment of every day.

One night after the trestle tables had been put away and everyone was soundly asleep on pallets on the straw-covered, dirt floor, Egar awoke to someone shaking his shoulder.

"Shhh." Gisela held a finger to her lips, motioning him to follow.

Puzzled he grabbed his cloak and tiptoed after her. Leaving the inn, they hurried silently down the lane and into a black alley. She stopped before a building and opened a door so dark he could not see the handle.

The room was unlit except for a small fire in a brazier. Crocks and containers lined the shelves. Bunches of herbs hung from the rafters. Standing in the shadows behind the fire was an old man dressed in a long dark robe. The entire scene was so reminiscent of the cave that Egar felt immediately at home.

Gisela went to kneel at the man's feet to receive a blessing sign over her head and a touch on her shoulder. The priest turned to gaze at Egar.

"Who sent you?"

"Sent? I do not understand," responded Egar, puzzled.

"Who was your teacher?"

"Oh. I... I only knew him as 'Master'."

"Picture him for me."

"Picture?"

"Here, lad. Sit." The priest pointed to a bench before the brazier.

Egar sat, gazing involuntarily into the flame. He was astounded to find the familiar face of his old master staring at him from the fire. Silence quivered, taut with magic. There was an instant memory of words his master had spoken at their parting.

"Will I see you?"

"In your mind's eye, and occasionally in a dream or the smoke and flame of a fire."

His master's message took on new significance. Egar wondered what truth his promise of destiny might bear as well.

"Can I speak with him?"

The priest peered intently over Egar's shoulder. "No. You may but observe."

Egar was disappointed. "Can he see me?"

"Only if he is looking for you."

The harsh lines of the priest's face softened. "You were right to bring him, Gisela. He was sent. You may go, my child. Our friend has much to do this night."

Gisela bowed and left.

The priest turned to Egar. "You have been sent by one who knows. Whether you take up the burden placed upon you by the gods is a decision you alone can make."

"Oh, I will!" exclaimed Egar.

"It is not easy," the priest cautioned. "Your commitment and endurance will be tested. Only if you succeed will you be accepted into our brotherhood. Do you choose to undertake the challenge now, tonight?"

Egar was breathless at the speed with which his life was changing. He needed time to prepare. But he might not be given another chance.

"Yes. I will do whatever you ask of me."

"Good. Stand here." The priest directed Egar to a place about half-way between the brazier and the wall.

The priest, chanting words Egar could not understand, took chalk and drew a circle on the floor around where he stood. He intersected that circle with a triangle.

When finished, the priest stood. "You must stand within these sacred confines until dawn reveals the walls of this room. Although drawn on the floor, you must observe their boundaries straight up from where they are. If any part of your body extends beyond the spiritual wall surrounding you, the trial will be terminated and you are free to leave. You will simply be denied admittance into our brotherhood and the lessons of the henge. Do you understand?"

"Yes."

"You will be alone. No one will watch you. But you do understand, we will know if the boundaries have been broken?"

"Yes."

"Good. One more thing. This test must be accomplished in silence. You are not to talk, sing, nor chant. Neither are you to create sound by hitting your body or stamping your feet. I leave you now and hope with all my heart to find you here at dawn."

Thoughts of the strange things happening to him swirled in Egar's head. He knew not what part his capture by the outlaws played in his destiny. Only that his master's words resounded with truth and wisdom. Something awaited him in the darkness beyond the chamber. A plan for his life?

The test seemed simple enough. Standing was not uncomfortable. He looked around the room, trying to identify the herbs, potions, and objects with which it was cluttered, but the fire in the brazier had gone out, leaving barely glowing coals. Walls and ceiling receded into shadows.

Egar decided perhaps the worst part of the test would be the boredom of standing by himself in a dark space. He thought about Gisela, recalling the magic of their lovemaking. As he relived the afternoon in Stonehenge he felt his loins harden. The stimulation gave Egar, whose attention had begun to flag, a gratifying boost.

If he could keep his erection, there was no doubt in his mind, dawn would find him wide awake and standing well within the confines of his inviolate space. Unfortunately his hardness began to fail. He could bring back neither its stimulation nor any mental image of Gisela. He was alone.

As the night wore on, his feet and legs began to ache. His eyes longed to close. Sleep, whether he willed it or not, was waiting to claim him.

A sudden prickling sensation jolted him awake. Something moved with stealth along the shelves. Faint sounds of squeaking and scratching pricked his ears. Rats! One of them, at least a full hand's span and more in length crept up to the magic marks on the floor. It stared at Egar, its eyes reflecting the glowing embers in the brazier.

The huge rodent was not in the least afraid. Egar held his breath, waiting for the scruffy thing to penetrate his sacred space. He could imagine sharp teeth dripping with blood. If it were not for the prohibition on sound he would have tried shouting to frighten it away. As it was, all Egar could do was stare back into those sinister red eyes. Finally the rat grew tired of a figure that did not move and left to join the pack rummaging about the room.

Egar became aware of the chill creeping across the floor. Relentlessly it rose up his legs, entered his body, climbed the ladder of his backbone. He shivered involuntarily. He hugged his arms across his chest to preserve what little heat he could. He gazed longingly at his cloak hung carelessly on a peg near the door. If only he could break out of his prison to grab it, feel its warmth.

The urge to stretch out his arms as wide as they would go was almost unbearable. He longed to sit, to—oh heavenly thought—lie down on his soft warm palet with the blanket tucked around his neck. He tortured himself with thoughts of comfort beyond his reach.

But, Egar thought, instead of fighting my body's urges, I should use my skills to leave it and put myself at ease. He began to construct the framework which would allow him to leave his aching person behind. The body, bereft of the control that thought exerted, began to weave and nearly toppled over. Egar jumped back into his skin and bones, barely avoiding breaking the forbidden barrier.

He took stock. His feet and legs were painfully numb. His eyes felt as though sand had been thrown in them. With each blink, keeping them open seemed more unendurable. His teeth were covered with the fuzz of night, his mouth tasted foully of onions, eaten long since. His back ached and his ears rang with a persistent high-pitched humming. Oh to be allowed to sleep.

Egar massaged his scalp and cheeks, always monitoring that his elbows did not invade the forbidden space beyond the lines on the floor. It felt wonderful to bring feeling to those areas and for a moment he was awake and content.

He bent his knees slightly, moved his eyes from right to left, up and down, rubbed his neck and shoulders.

He kept himself awake by inflicting pain. Pulled out strands of his own hair. Dug his nails into his palms. Drew blood.

He thought fleetingly of sending a thought out into the night, begging his master for help, but discarded it immediately. This was his trial. Succeess or failure was his alone to earn.

While searching for anything he could do to keep his senses alert he realized the room was infinitesimally lighter. He could see beyond his enclosure!

The silent, unmoving forms of robed priests emerged from the deep shadows. Egar wondered, how they had entered without his being aware of it. How long had they been there? How much of his struggle had they observed? When Egar realized he could see the walls of the room, he almost fainted with relief!

A low humming, like bees swarming from far off, filled the air. The humming grew louder as the priests broke into a chant. They repeated unintelligible syllables over and over, subtly changing the interweaving harmonies. As the hymn grew more insistent, Egar recognized it as a song of praise. For the new day? Or his success?

The priest helped him step outside the marks. "You have done well, my son. We are proud of you. Each of us has undergone the same ordeal. We know well what it requires."

His mentor looked around to the others, each of whom nodded gravely. "You will stand with us in Stonehenge on midsummer's eve."

Chapter Five

Twelve priests stood in the darkness. Egar among them, felt the stirring of great wisdom just beyond the horizon of his understanding.

The origins of Stonehenge were lost beyond anyone's knowledge—the stones old when the Romans came. No one knew who built them. Nor how. Nor why. Priests in those long forgotten days must have known how to read the heavenly bodies as if they were words written by the gods. Been able to calculate not only the days of solstice and equinox, but eclipses of the sun and moon as well.

To Egar, it seemed the stars overhead moved at an accelerated pace, making majestic music of the universe as they wheeled about the heavens. The gray-robed figures about him looked like small copies of the giant standing stones casting deep shadows in the moonlight.

For a timeless instant Egar held the thought like a crystal: Though humans were not meant to understand their fate, they might, if the gods willed it, receive a glimpse that everything was ordered.

A breeze fluttered the robes about his feet. The sky in the east was a shade lighter. The moon sank majestically toward the west.

The first ray of the mid-summer sun gleamed at the edge of the horizon. It shot, like a spear, straight down the opening between the standing stones to illuminate the altar. There it met, as fingers that touch in parting, the cold gleam of the setting moon. Egar felt a stir of emotion to have been chosen to witness the event.

The figures of the priests melted into the early morning shadows. Taking off their robes, they separated, to make their way silently to homes and farms.

Egar looked for Gisela. He was anxious to share with her the feelings aroused by this night. The expectation of being with her filled him with excitement. But she was not there.

Unable to find her, he followed his mentor priest who neatly folded his robe into the bottom of his travel sack. On top of it he began gathering healing herbs still blessed with morning dew. At last they stopped under the shade of a tree.

Egar stretched out on the grass. He was tired after the long night of standing in the henge but too excited to sleep.

After a period of silence the priest spoke. "What did you learn this past night?"

Egar thought back to the moment when the sun's rays pierced through the opening between the huge stones.

"I learned the universe was created by the gods with awesome exactitude. Every moment of the day and night, even sun and stars follow their assigned paths."

"And in what way does this lesson apply to you?"

"Me?" Egar pondered the question. "Is there a place in the plan of the universe apportioned by the gods to me?"

"A conceivable idea. You would be wise to think on it as you live your life. Did you learn aught else?"

Egar lay with his chin cupped in his palm. "Until now I have acknowledged the alternating of daylight and darkness, the cycle of the seasons, but have thought of them only in terms of the present moment. During the night I felt the weight of ages past. It was the first time I have thought of times before I was alive... and that there will be a future beyond my death. It is a strange idea."

"And one to consider," agreed the priest.

"Is it true, in ancient times men had the skill and knowledge to unlock the secrets of the gods?" asked Egar.

"It must be. Else how and why did they build the henge?"

"Do you share their knowledge?"

"Alas, no. We are only the keepers of the dream. We must remember that such knowledge is possible. There will come a time when man will unlock the secrets of the universe once again. Until then we keep the idea of such thoughts alive."

"Like the person who banks the coals to keep the ember alive, so later the fire might burn," Egar cried.

"Well said!"

Egar glowed with pleasure at the praise.

The priest continued quietly, "You have been chosen to serve the gods. As were we and those of old."

Egar felt his face flush at the thought of being so honored.

"You must leave. Your destiny beckons," continued the priest. "You have been shown the wonders necessary for your understanding."

Egar sat up. "Go? I thought to stay yet a while. And Gisela..."

"Her place is not with you. Your time together was a precious gift of the gods. They are not usually so generous. Now you must do their bidding."

Egar nodded, mutely, not trusting his voice. Finally he asked, "May I see her to say good-bye?"

"It is better you do not. Of all the kinds of pain in this life, parting from someone you love—whether in death, circumstance or duty—is the hardest to bear."

Egar bowed his head.

He searched in his bag and found a drop of amber with an insect caught, perfect and life-like as if in a golden drop of honey. "Will you give her this gift to remember me by?"

The priest gently took the amber from Egar. "Gisela needs no gift to remember you. You are as embedded in her memory as is this insect in the amber. But I will see she receives this keepsake from your heart.

"Now go. Look not back. Go forward with courage to meet your destiny."

"But where? In what direction? I knew not I was to come here. I ran away, heedless of anything but to save my life. And yet... I was expected. Where next should I go?"

In a gesture reminiscent of the master, the priest lightly laid a hand on Egar's head and gazed into the distance.

"Britain's legend has come and gone but it will live on in poetry and song. Frankish Gaul's legend has yet to be but once come, in history's chronicles will it known forever be."

Egar wondered what this vague message meant and how it might direct his steps. He knew he would get no explanation. He sighed, his emotions too raw to puzzle it further.

"Though the forces for evil be strong," continued the priest, "you can influence that which works for good if you fail not the challenges of your destiny."

Egar did not even try to fathom what influence he might have. He could hardly remember the exaltation of Stonehenge. The night past seemed but a strange and distant dream. Reality was the sharp-edged pain of parting from Gisela, without so much as one more look, one more embrace.

Depression settled on his shoulders like an unwanted mantle.

Egar rode in a daze. He noticed neither the bright summer sun beating on his bent back nor the sudden coolness when the road wound into a deep forest. As daylight faded into murky dusk a rustle and crashing ahead brought him to his senses. A wild animal dashed across the narrow path, plunging into the underbrush as it continued on its mad course. Egar's horse reared nearly unseating him. He at last realized darkness precluded further travel.

The gods had not entirely forgotten him. A cave barely visible in the gathering gloom offered shelter of a sort.

Without thought, Egar gathered dried moss, leaves and sticks to start a fire. To his chagrin, no flame began licking at the tinder-dry kindling. How could this be? Starting a fire was one of the first feats of magic he had learned. Magicians with even the smallest gift used starting a fire as a trick to amaze onlookers. Egar concentrated, step by step, for the first time in many years.

Not the slightest change. No glow of heat. No wisp of smoke curling upward. He had lost even the small power necessary for this simple task. With a black humor Egar rubbed a stick round and round to create a spark, in the age-old way of ordinary men.

Later that evening he gazed into the flame of the small fire that finally illuminated the mouth of his cave. Vainly he searched for Gisela's gentle face in the smoke and flame.

He realized neither his master nor the priest had mates. Was celibacy required of those chosen to serve the gods? Surely that was asking too much!

In desperation Egar tried to bring the likeness of his master into the fire. It eluded him as did that of the priest. The gods had taken back their gift. Bitter tears welled and a painful lump grew in his throat making it impossible to swallow.

Would his destiny be a blessing or a curse?

Egar had no idea how long he remained curled in a ball on the floor of the cave. He slept deeply at first, exhausted from the night at Stonehenge followed by the turmoil of being sent out again on his own. Now he hung, suspended halfway between slumber and wakefulness.

In the darkness of another night, long after he had given up any hope of it, Egar suddenly saw Gisela. Her blue eyes were filled with a longing that matched his own. Though the night was chill, she wore no cloak.

She spoke no word but Egar heard her every thought.

"Come," she said as if she had spoken aloud.

He felt the weight of depression lift and was overcome by a sense of lightness. No longer pinned to the floor of the cave, he and Gisela rose into the star-spangled sky sailing far above the Narrow Sea.

Side by side, Gisela and Egar soared over the dark and featureless land beyond the sea. They came upon a river, a silver ribbon winding through the black void below. Egar wanted to go on and on forever, following the thread of moon-dappled water, Gisela at his side. He felt like turning somersaults among the stars.

They hovered like hawks riding the wind currents, over an island in the middle of the river. Egar saw torch lights flickering in the darkness. He realized he must come again to this glittering isle.

"Come with me," he bid Gisela. "Live with me here."

His words flew on and on into empty space, like a stone skipping across a lake. Egar knew he was alone again. Not only alone, but returned in the blink of an eye to his solitary cave somewhere in the trackless forest a day's journey from Stonehenge and his love.

Though his heart was breaking, Egar knew if he could not have Gisela, he must return to the land of the

Franks and find the island city which she had shown him. He had no idea how to find the magic island. He wondered fleetingly whether there actually was such a place in the real world, or if it were a mystical symbol for some destiny he could neither grasp nor understand.

Chapter Six

Precious months slipped by as Egar earned his way back across the Narrow Sea. The warm days of summer and flaming weeks of fall were spent. Now driving rain soaked through his moss-colored traveling cloak, burying the cold deep into his bones.

His horse had injured its leg and Egar was forced to walk through thick mud that clung to every step. His feet were blue with cold and wet breeches rubbed against his thighs raising angry, burning welts.

The clouds were so low he could see no more than a few paces ahead or behind where he and the animals were the only occupants of the road.

Egar had no idea how much farther in the distance Paris lay. He only knew if he followed the Seine River long enough, eventually he would reach the island city. It was the only one he had heard of that might be the town of Gisela's vision. He strove onward, the thought of spending one more night out in weather like this, driving him to put one foot in front of the other.

The sun's last feeble light seeped out from beneath the clouds as Egar finally approached the wall of a stone monastery on the Left Bank of the Seine. Bells tolled Vespers as he approached.

"Have you a place where I can rest my animals?" he asked of the brother closing the massive wooden gates. "I am cold and wet. If we can but stay the night, tomorrow I will look for lodging in Paris."

"If you are willing to share our humble quarters and frugal meal," the brother replied, "you are welcome."

In a rude stable, Egar rubbed both animals dry with handfuls of hay. He cleaned the horse's hoof, spreading on a healing salve.

Carrying his pack, Egar followed the monk to a cell. A pallet on which to sleep and a crucifix on the wall were all the niche contained. Egar shivered as he stripped off his sopping clothes. The rough wool robe left by the monk felt wonderfully warm.

Except that his head wasn't tonsured, Egar looked no different than the other monks as they took their places at the long bare trestle table in the refectory. One of the friars gave the blessing. The monks ate silently while a brother read aloud from the scriptures. Egar's serving of hard bread and bowl of warm soup tasted like food from a king's table. They disappeared into his hunger without a trace. He soon realized that was all any of them were to get. It would have to be enough.

Egar slept like the dead from the moment his head touched the pallet. He did not hear the bell tolling midnight nor the rustle of monks walking softly into the sanctuary to observe Matins with worship and prayer.

Some time later a vision of Gisela came to him again. The sight of her filled him with longing.

She was dressed in the white robe of a priestess and he understood she was to enter an enclave where they worshiped the old gods. Once accepted, she would never leave.

Egar cried out in silence, "You cannot go! I need hope we can be together again, someday."

He drank in the sight of her as if parched with thirst. He had never wanted anything so much as he did the feel of her body against his.

She neither responded, nor looked away.

"Go, my love," he offered at last. "You are more precious to me than life. But how can I ask you to deny your destiny while I search to discover my own?"

A look of overwhelming love filled her eyes, caressing him one last time. Then, without a backward glance she walked toward a golden light. Egar watched, tears streaming down his cheeks, until she disappeared, doubtlessly forever.

Early the next morning Egar led the limping palfrey and his laden mule out the monastery gate. Nearby a bridge led to the île de la Cité. The rain had stopped and a thin sun groped its way through the early morning mist. Paris floated above the river in a chilly sea of vapor.

Entering the city, Egar was attracted by shouting. A crowd, gathered around a tall wooden post in the center of an open square, cheered on some activity inside their circle. The horde seemed to be made up of peasants wearing worn and dirty rags. Many were barefoot on this frigid morning. One old crone laughed uproariously, showing a mouth full of broken, rotting teeth.

The people shifted and Egar got his first sight of the sport that so entertained them. A live cat was nailed to the post. In agonizing pain and thoroughly frightened, its fur was matted and sticky with blood. Opposing the animal was a lad of perhaps ten or eleven in filthy drawers and tattered shirt. His tangled hair stuck out in all directions. His hands were tied behind his back and he was trying to butt the cat to death with his head. The beast's sharp claws and needle-like teeth lashed out at him in a frenzy.

Egar froze when the cat swiped the boy's face, tearing the skin in a long jagged slash from temple to chin, missing his eye by a hairsbreadth. Blinded by spurts of blood, the boy nearly as terrified as the cat, pounded the animal with his head. The blow mercifully put the poor creature out of its misery.

The onlookers shouted in triumph. They had enjoyed the exciting duel. Someone began binding the boy's bleeding head with a dirty rag, while he grasped eagerly at the few coins wagered on the outcome. For these he had risked permanent blindness and paid dearly with the ugly disfiguring of an otherwise unremarkable peasant face.

Egar looked at the milling crowd. He thought his family could easily have been any of these people. They were not, of course. They lived nowhere near Paris. But they had the same brutish lack of concern for suffering and death.

Egar swallowed against the bile that rose at the sight of such wanton pain and death. He felt alien once again. He had no idea why he would rather mend a bird's broken wing than stone it to death, nor what defect in his character made him unable to fit into the family of his birth. He was overcome with a feeling of disorientation.

The excitement over, everyone walked off ignoring the mangled carcass of the cat hanging on the post. Egar could do nothing for the dead cat. Or himself.

Unused to such crowds, his senses were assaulted by the sights, sounds and stench of the city. The streets were paved with stones in the Roman manner. The noise of wheels rumbling over the cobbles and the cries of pedlars calling their wares rang in his ears.

He passed two men building a home. Matting woven from sticks and reeds was placed in square areas between wooden beams. One man daubed clay over the matting to strengthen and seal it. There was hardly an arms-length between this and the other wattle and daub, thatch-topped huts. Their yards were barely large enough for a small vegetable garden, a cesspit, and chicken coop or pig sty.

Egar looked in vain for open fields or patches of green. He wondered how people could live amid such crowds and clamor. He doubted this was the magical city Gisela had shown him. He would but winter here and continue his search come spring.

At the westernmost tip of the island he confronted a palisade of tightly-packed logs. A flow of soldiers on horseback and peasants on foot passed in and out the open gate. Egar realized this must be a royal residence of the Merovingian king.

Inside, the bailey or open yard of the palace compound was dominated by a rectangular wooden two-storied structure. It was made of the same tightly-spaced logs as the outer wall and seemed completely impregnable. This would be the great hall, center of all royal activities.

Men walked horses in and out the open double door of a large wooden stable or rode about the yard, exercising their mounts.

Egar could not tell whether the huts built against the palisade were homes for the people of King Clothar's court or workshops for skilled craftsmen attached to the palace.

The blacksmith stood at an open-fronted shed. The fire looked warm and inviting, but the steady ring of his hammer discouraged conversation.

In one corner of the yard a group of soldiers practiced throwing axes. Egar watched wide-eyed as one after the other stood behind a mark on the ground and hurled his weapon whistling through the air to land with a deep 'thwack' in the giant stump of a tree serving as target. No wonder the Franks and their swift axes were so feared in a fight!

The aroma of baking bread and roasting meats drew Egar to the kitchen building. His mouth watered and his stomach growled, reminding him how little he had eaten at the abbey. He followed the delectable smells to the kitchen door.

"By the Three, get thee gone thee thieving scoundrel," cried the cook wiping her roughened red hands on a voluminous apron.

In all fairness, he did look the beggar. This morning ice covered the water in the trough at the monastery, making it easy to dispense with washing face and hands. And his travel clothes were still damp with mud.

"I can earn my keep," Egar protested.

He ducked under the fleshy arm extended to bar his way. With his most engaging smile, he grabbed an armful of potatoes from a sack on the floor and immediately started juggling them around his head. The cook watched in open-mouthed fascination.

Seeing he had her undivided attention, Egar traded the potatoes for a half dozen fresh eggs nestled in a basket on the work table.

"By all the saints, put them precious eggs down. Thee'll muddle the yolks and break all the shells. They be meant for the king's pudding. I'll skin thee alive, thou addelpated knave."

Before she had finished scolding, helplessly waving her thick arms in the air, five of the eggs had successfully found their way back to the basket without so much as a hairline crack to mark their amazing adventure.

Egar felt quite cocky at the cook's admiring glance. He gave the last egg a jaunty twist and—gasped as it missed it's place in the basket, landing instead with a splat on top of his boot. He stared as the yellow yolk quivered then seeped out to swim in the clear slime surrounding it.

Egar's cheeks flamed in embarrassment. Why must he show off? Now he had lost his chance to earn a meal.

He quickly bent down trying to erase his blunder. There was nothing he could do about the interior of the egg. It was too slippery to pick up. Egar grabbed the cracked shell and tossed it into a rubbish heap in the corner.

"Stop, thou empty-headed oaf!" The cook grabbed back the eggshell. "By all the sweet saints in heaven, be thee completely witless? How does thee suppose the wood sprites get into the castle with all the thresholds blest I ask thee? Every simpleton knows they make air boats of uncrushed eggshells and sail in through the windows." So saying, she carefully crumbled the shell into tiny bits.

"I meant no harm. I have no coins now. But when I earn some, I will return and pay for the broken egg. I promise..."

"All right, all right!" The cook looked heavenward. "Sweet Mary, give me strength! Thee can stable thy pathetic animals in the building, yonder, and bed thyself down in the hay beside them. I will speak to Chucus about thy amazing talents. As Mayor of the Palace *he* can decide whether to feed thee or hang thee for thy knavery."

She pushed Egar out the kitchen door, whacking him smartly on the rump with a huge wooden spoon, her badge of office as cook to the court. At the same time, she gave him a half loaf of dark bread and nearly a whole sausage. During all of this she never stopped scolding in a loud voice that rang through the kitchen and out into the yard.

Egar grinned from ear to ear. He had won her favor with his brash performance. To be on the cook's good side was next best to the king's. Allowing himself a small swagger he walked to the stable, wolfing his food as he went.

Chapter Seven

Two nights later, an entirely different Egar stood poised at the threshold of the great hall. Food, rest, and a basin of warm water had wrought a minor miracle. Not just his face and hands, but his hair as well was freshly washed. Over his linen shirt he wore the brilliant green, loose, sleeveless mantle which he saved for special occasions. His thigh-high woolen stockings were a darker green laced with bands of brightest yellow.

The great hall was the largest room he had ever seen. Egar closed his eyes for a moment, praying he would not embarrass himself by making a stupid mistake. He thought of his egg-splattered boot. Spurred by disgrace he had spent the past two days practicing for his performance at court.

The huge room buzzed with conversations. The air was filled with expectation. Entertainment was more than agreeable, especially as winter lengthened the evenings. Torches placed into holders on the walls illuminated the scene with their flickering light. The king and queen having finished their supper, lounged in carved wooden thrones at their table on the raised dais. Members of the court relaxed on benches around long trestle tables. Servants, craftsmen and soldiers stood or sat on benches placed against the outside walls. Smoke drifting from the fire lay across the room like an opaque blanket.

Egar stepped into the hall. It smelled, as usual, of crushed straw, decayed meat dropped on the way to some nobleman's mouth, a discarded bone or two, and perhaps a dead mouse brought in by a proud feline. Also, with the weather turned chill, no one would think about bathing again until May or June, so it smelled of unwashed flesh as well.

Egar was aware of none of this, so intent was he on the figure of the king. After bowing, he looked expectantly for some sign that this was indeed the beginning of his destiny. Blue eyes and long blond hair. What had he expected?

Covering his disappointment, Egar turned to the court. First he ceremoniously opened a flat, oblong box. The great hall grew silent as everyone strained to see what was inside.

Egar paced around the table showing the six identical hunting knives that lay within. To prove the sharpness of the blades, Egar turned to a young page holding a platter of roast mutton. Quickly he sliced off several parchment-thin portions, gallantly handing them to the ladies to nibble.

Then he laid the knives on the end of the table in a neat row. Carefully he picked up one knife and tossed it into the air. It went up, spinning blade over handle to the top of its arch, then tumbled downward. Egar caught it by the handle and sent it up again. Without pause to look where the rest of the knives lay on the table, Egar picked up a second knife and sent it upward with his left hand as he caught the first with his right. If he were to miss and catch a knife by the blade instead of the handle it would cut his hand deeply, spilling blood and crippling his fingers. This feat required all his skill and concentration.

The assembled crowd gasped as he picked up a third and fourth knife, sending two into the air as he caught the two that fell almost simultaneously. Egar did not hear their quick intake of breath. He focused all of his attention on the knives. Soon he had six knives in the smoky air. Everyone watched the sharp edges with suspended breath.

Without a blink, Egar caught one knife and gave it an extra flip. As he continued with the other five, the first one went spinning out of orbit and into the table, landing point-first and quivering to a stop, upright, the tip buried in the wood. In quick succession the other five knives followed suit, until all were standing at attention, tips interred in the table top.

At last both Egar and the court were able to breathe again. He wiped the perspiration from his brow and bowed to enthusiastic cheers. Egar smiled. He had captured the favor of his royal audience!

Egar's eye was caught by the king's ring.

"Sire, may I see your ring more closely?" he asked.

Clothar held out his hand for Egar's inspection.

"May I?" he asked, touching the flashing green emerald.

"I suppose so." The king handed the ring to Egar. "But take care. It is valued at more than your life is worth. And it is a particular favorite of mine, as well."

Putting it on his own hand, Egar walked around the table again so everyone could see the beauty of the stone, wrapped in a serpent of twisted gold. The ring was an extraordinary ornament, so large it would have taken at least one and a half of Egar's fingers to wear it safely. As he returned to the head table, his hand moved quickly and the ring disappeared!

Egar searched for it in the folds and pockets of his mantle. It was not there. Perhaps it had fallen on the table, the floor, into the lap of a nearby nobleman or his lady? Everyone began looking for the royal gem. The king looked as dismayed as Egar.

Distractedly Egar handed the king a basket of shiny apples. The monarch selected one that was perfect in every way, without cut or blemish. As unheeding as Egar had been, the king picked up his hunting knife to slit open the apple to eat and found his own emerald ring nestled among the seeds of its core! The room erupted in shouts of approval. Egar had convinced them all the ring was lost. Everyone stamped and clapped in relief and surprise. Fortunately the king seemed to enjoy the joke as much as the rest.

"By Mithras!" cried the king. "You must come back again to entertain. Where is your home, lad?"

"With my horse and pack mule in your stable."

"Have we not room in the palace for this wonderful magician?" asked the king.

"He can sleep with the servants, the craftsmen, and their families here on the floor tonight," the queen replied. "Perhaps tomorrow we could find an alcove where his paraphernalia will come to no harm."

If I have not found my destiny, Egar thought to himself, I have at least found a royal roof over my head and a place, albeit below the salt, at the royal table.

Egar's alcove was just off the great hall. A leather curtain provided privacy from the many people who ate and slept there. His clothes hung on pegs inside the doorway. A small table held pitcher and basin, a chamber pot beneath. His saddle bags and baskets filled the space between it and the pallet bed along the wall.

He was supremely happy. How could someone born into a dark villein's hut feel so comfortable in the palace of the King of All Franks? Even the pages were sons of noble birth. He pondered what effect his own humble beginnings might have on his destiny. Why was it both the master and the priest felt he had been somehow chosen by the gods?

A memory of the squalid home he had left when he wandered to the Master's cave filled his head. Why had his family cared so little for him, they had allowed him to wander off? He felt an empty longing. Did they think of him? Had they loved him once?

He would likely never return to find out.

Having no idea how he came to be here, nor how long he would be welcome at court, Egar grinned as he re-lived his triumph of the previous night.

The queen stopped at his doorway to listen as Egar plucked his harp and sang.

"Would you come and sing for the ladies of the court in the chamber where we sit and do hand work? It would be a welcome relief for we grow weary of naught but our own company."

"I would be most happy. But someone will have to show me the way. I only know to find the great hall, the kitchen building and the stable."

The queen smiled. "A page will fetch you."

Egar was led up an inner stairway to a corner room. It was quite large as was necessary to accommodate the three looms at which ladies were throwing shuttles back and forth. Others sat on benches spinning, sewing and embroidering royal garments and ecclesiastical cloths. Egar tuned his harp and began to sing. The peddles on the looms kept time with the music.

After that Egar could be found there most afternoons singing ballads of fantasy and lost love. He taught the ladies to sing along. Their needles never paused nor did the shuttles lose a beat as high clear voices mingled with his tenor. In time they taught him favorites of their own. He took pleasure in learning them, thoroughly enjoying sharing the songs and happy to feel he had a part in the everyday life of the palace. His only fear was that soon they would tire of him and send him on his way.

He ate most of his meals at the far end of the tables with the pages and chambermaids, but once in a while was invited to dine further up among the nobles. On those evenings he entertained with juggling, magic and song.

He became a favorite with seven-year-old prince Dagobert and even taught him to catch one of the many colored balls he used in his juggling act. Before long, Dagobert could catch the thrown ball and return it with enough skill and accuracy that Egar could weave it into its place among the six or seven that were in the air all at one time. Egar and Dagobert performed their juggling act to the enthusiastic pleasure of the court.

After that success Dagobert was Egar's constant shadow. "Come to my lessons," he insisted. "I want you to meet my tutors Arnulf and Pepin."

Arnulf seemed reserved and off-putting. It was hard to believe that although tonsured and wearing the simple, coarse robe of a monk, he was actually the Bishop of Metz.

Egar was immediately taken with Pepin. Tall and muscular, he radiated energy. His reddish hair seemed to have a life of its own. While King Clothar and his son had a fragile beauty, Pepin was coarser but perfectly proportioned. Where the royal eyes were the blue of an early morning's sky, Pepin's were the color of the ocean at midday.

"Welcome." Pepin grasped Egar's hand. "Come to see the young prince at his lessons, have you?"

"If I may, sir," replied Egar.

"Of course. Everyone in the court is welcome."

Half a dozen students, children of the mayor of the palace and other high ranking officials were in the class, though none said a word while Dagobert was in attendance.

"Well, Dagobert, shall I be the teacher or you today?" asked Pepin.

"You ask. I know all the answers." The proud prince was happy to show off for his new hero.

"Very well, why do you learn to read?"

"In order to understand the Holy Scriptures," came the prompt reply.

"And why learn to scribe?"

"In order to make more copies of them."

"Why do you learn numbers?"

"In order to keep accounts and be certain everyone pays the right taxes to me when I grow up to be king."

"Is all learning for some utilitarian purpose?" asked Egar. "Is nothing learned for the sheer joy of understanding more of this amazing world today than you did yesterday?"

"Ah, that depends upon the learner," Pepin replied. "For young Dagobert here, all learning is functional in becoming a well-trained monarch who can control and expand his kingdom. But that is because he already knows his destiny.

"You, on the other hand, may still be trying to discover yours. All knowledge might in time find its place in your life. So all learning is welcome, immediately useful or not."

Egar was amazed at Pepin's perceptiveness.

When Dagobert ran out to take his riding lesson, Pepin invited Egar to come with him to his own apartments where he lived with his wife, Itta, and toddler son, Grimwald.

When they entered, little Grimwald's face lit with glee. A miniature version of Pepin, he waddled to his father on fat, bowed legs. Pepin tossed his son high in the air. The child shrieked with laughter.

Itta rested on a couch. A patrician beauty, she had dark hair and eyes, and a regal nose. Her complexion, however, was sallow with dark smudges under her eyes. Her posture suggested exhaustion.

Upon being presented, Egar blurted, "Madam, my old master has taught me something of the healing arts. Perhaps I might have in my pack an herb or two that would settle your stomach without harming the babe that grows within."

As if a thunderbolt had split the room, everyone froze in place. Egar felt a moment's panic. Then all started talking at once.

"How could you know I am with child, since I, myself, did not even suspect it?" asked Itta. "Though it would explain why I have been unable to retain even the mildest of pottage."

"Lad, have you the gift of sight?" Pepin's query conveyed apprehension.

"I know not how I spoke thus," stammered Egar. "My master told me the sight would come with time and experience. If it is a gift, I know not why it came just now as it did."

"Well, time will tell whether it is a true gift or not," said Pepin. "About nine months, I would wager."

"Please, sir, tell no one." Fear tightened Egar's stomach and made his heart race. "People mistrust that which they do not understand. And if *I* can not understand, how could anyone else?"

"Have no fear," assured Pepin.

Egar's potion soothed Itta's delicate digestion, and a few weeks later she confirmed his gift. She was with child.

Chapter Eight

One evening, just past the new year, Egar began to entertain with a few feats of magic as he often did. But, in the middle of a sleight of hand, he saw something that caused him to drop the golden cage, letting loose a dozen previously unseen white doves to fly around the hall. He looked at Pepin, unable to believe his eyes.

He felt the oppressive silence in the great hall. Knew he was the center of puzzled attention. Could do nothing but stare, transfixed. When mutters began among the on-lookers, Egar, with extraordinary effort, pulled his eyes away. Mumbling an apology, he collected himself and continued his act. Distracted, he performed poorly.

Afterward, his mind raced like a frenzied thing. Methodically he put away the paraphernalia of his magic tricks. Interconnected rings which only he knew how to separate into one of the baskets. The bird cage with its nearly invisible false bottom in the space beside his bed. I will have to catch the doves all over again, he thought, avoiding the vision he could not put out of his mind.

Pepin strode in. "What happened? You looked at me as if I were a stranger and terrible to behold."

"In truth, for a moment when I looked at you... that is just what it seemed."

"Tell me what you saw."

"I know not what I should disclose."

"Does it affect me?" queried Pepin.

"I can not tell with certainty but it might *be* you."

"Well, then, tell me. Is it awful?"

"Full of awe. But wonderful. Not bad."

"By the gods, boy, tell me. What did you see?"

"I saw a future king. Though he, I..."

Pepin seemed about to shake the information from Egar. Then stopped and walked about the cramped space of the alcove pounding his fist into his hand.

"I saw a king dressed in royal finery with a long blue mantle that matched his eyes," said Egar breathlessly. "He wore a wrought gold circlet about his red-blond hair. The whole scene was illumined with a glow of unearthly light. At that instant I knew—though I know not how—he was to be the greatest king of all time."

"By all the living gods, what has this to do with me?"

"I could not see the features plainly but it happened when I looked at you. I can think of no other explanation. You *might* become the king of my vision!"

Pepin smiled. To Egar it seemed as if something Pepin had been born knowing, or long ago guessed, had just been confirmed.

Pepin was elated but also thoroughly shaken. He knew, as Egar probably did not, that since the time of Clovis, well over a hundred years ago, no one had been king of the Franks except those born of the Merovingian line. Pepin was well-connected and had a high place at court, a trusted advisor to the king and tutor to the prince. But that he should aspire to be king himself was beyond all reason. And yet...

Gripping Egar's arm, Pepin whispered fiercely, "Tell no one what you have seen this night. No one! If

Clothar hears so much as a whisper, he will kill me. Have no doubt, you will suffer as well."

"The secret is safe with me. I know not what to make of it at any rate."

"By all the gods, it had better be. Clothar is genial enough now that he is king of all Franks. But he would put down any threat to his throne, swiftly and cruelly. I know what I say. Remember what he did to Brundhilde less than five years ago."

"I have not heard of that. News of the court seldom traveled as far as our solitary cave in the hills. Who was Brundhilde and what did Clothar do?"

"Brundhilde was Clothar's aunt and rival for the throne of the province of Burgundy," said Pepin. "She was the oldest person in all the realm and served as regent for her infant great-grandson, Sigibert. Then Clothar decided he wanted Burgundy for himself.

"There was no real fight. The nobles and soldiers had already thrown their support to Clothar's side," Pepin continued. "But the old she-witch would not give in, so Clothar killed the infant king and then..."

"What did he do?" Egar's eyes were huge.

"I can remember it as if it were but yesterday," said Pepin, more to himself than to Egar. "Brundhilde came down to where we were assembled on a field near her palace. She was dressed in her finest royal gown. I was surprised, old as she was—nearly 70—she stood up to all of us, her eyes blazing with defiance. It must have dismayed her to see Arnulf and me along with her mayor of the palace, all sworn to Clothar.

"Clothar called out for all to hear, 'Brundhilde, regent, leader, queen, I charge you with actions that have caused the deaths of ten Frankish kings.'

"No one stirred. The sun beat down. A slight breeze caught at Brundhilde's mantle and it billowed out around her feet. The only sound was that of the horses snorting and shifting weight from one hoof to the other.

"Clothar did not mention how many Frankish kings his own mother, Fredegund, had caused to die," Pepin added. His energy filled the alcove to overflowing.

Egar stood spell-bound in one corner of the chamber. "These Merovingians seem a blood-thirsty lot. What happened next?"

"Clothar ordered an unbroken horse brought to where he and Brundhilde stood. I remember the soft muttering of the soldiers wondering what was about to happen.

"An untamed stallion was brought in. Clothar's voice rang out again, 'Brundhilde, enemy of the provinces of Austrasia, Neustria and Burgundy, I condemn you to death, tied to this wild stallion!'

"She cried out, 'No! You cannot do this to a queen!' She struggled briefly but her strength was no match for the men who grabbed her hair, her right arm and right leg and began tying them to the frightened animal's tail."

"How ghastly!" Egar's face was blanched white.

"She had stood with dignity before us," Pepin continued. "But that was completely taken away as her robes blew about revealing spindly legs and arms flailing impotently against the ropes binding her to the horse.

"Clothar shouted, as he hit the stallion's flank.

"Brundhilde cried out in pain when the sharp hooves cut into her body. Her hair and pinioned limbs were pulled by the horse's tail. Her untied leg hit the ground and broke with a snap. Her body bounced between the hard ground and the pounding hooves.

"After what seemed a very long time her wild shrieks finally stopped. In the ensuing silence the beast slowed his panicked gallop to a trot, a walk, and finally stopped.

"Brundhilde's remains were burned and the ashes scattered." The event had the power to move Pepin even after all these years. "Clothar allowed no grave where her supporters could assemble and weep."

"What," inquired Egar, swallowing, "would you have done, had you been king?"

Pepin paused. Until now the idea was so unlikely he had never thought to question the king's decisions.

"Killing Sigibert was necessary," he said. "It was probably best he did it, himself, and quickly. Councils hesitate to kill infants, forgetting they grow up to become adults. Killing adults risks many lives at far greater cost.

"As for Brundhilde," Pepin shrugged, "perhaps she deserved her fate. At her age, I might have sent her to a nunnery. She had no more great-grandchildren and was no real threat. But I cannot fault Clothar for wanting to hurt her. The family feud had gone on for many years. She would have done the same or worse to him had their positions been reversed."

Egar shuddered. "I should think people would want someone who thought more of building the kingdom than of torture and murder, no matter his lineage."

"Most people care little that the Merovingians kill each other. As long as they have sons, the Franks will want kings with royal blood. Changing that will be the hardest part of fulfilling your vision. If it was a true one."

"It was a true vision—though perplexing."

Chapter Nine

Pepin kept tight rein on both his lips and temper, no mean feat for a man of his nature. But, in his mind he was preparing himself to fulfill Egar's prophecy and become the greatest king of all time. He viewed every situation, asking himself, 'What would I do if I were king?' Eventually, the *if* changed to *when*.

Pepin's preoccupation with his future changed his present. His new demeanor earned him the sobriquet, Pepin the Vain.

Egar had no further visions of Pepin's future or his own destiny. He became restless and was given to disappearing from time to time; no one ever saw him leave nor was anyone aware of his return.

"What about some entertainment tonight?"

"Has anyone seen Egar?"

"We could do with some sleight of hand and a ballad or two."

Egar was nowhere to be found. His old, moss-colored traveling cape was missing from the peg in the alcove where he slept, as was the bag in which he gathered healing herbs.

* * *

The first time Egar left, on a blustery March day a little over two months after his vision, was simply by chance. Perhaps the wind blowing fleecy clouds scudding through the cobalt sky made him fretful. Or he was unused to living in such close proximity to so many people.

He had grown up alone on a mountainside with his Old Master, who was often away. In the palace it seemed he was never alone; the air was always filled with man-made sounds.

Without any plan, Egar donned his drab cloak, the hood placing his face in shadows, and went for a walk. Looking for solitude, he left by a back, outside stairway that let him out behind the kitchen building. The cook was busy and did not notice as he walked quietly past the door.

Egar did not take his horse, his only desire to stroll in the fresh air to clear away the cobwebs and discontent that pervaded his spirit. But the streets of Paris, always crowded and noisy with carts and peddlers calling their wares, could not offer him the solace he craved.

He walked out the main gate and across the bridge in the company of others who were going the same way. It was not his plan to slip away inconspicuously. He simply joined the flow of people as unnoticing of others as he was unnoticed by them.

Once on the mainland he left the well-traveled road and followed the first track into the forest. After walking a good ways oblivious to his surroundings Egar slowed, feeling soothed by the spring air scented with moist earth and new green shoots. He could not remember the last time he had taken a breath that was not heavy with smoke and the odor of unwashed bodies and discarded food.

He was comforted to hear nothing but the chirping of birds and the rustle of still-bare branches moving in the capricious breeze. He turned his face to the warmth of the sunshine and stood, soaking up the fresh air and nature's sounds. In his mind's eye he saw Gisela, bathed in light, blue eyes filled with love. Not a vision one could reach out to. Not like the one he had seen of Pepin crowned king. Instead, it was the most pleasant of memories.

The longing, never far beneath the surface of his being, erupted with sudden force. He wanted to reach out and touch Gisela. To feel her, warm and responsive in his arms.

Would he be alone forever?

He let his feelings of loneliness flow to the surface where they gradually evaporated in the warmth of the sun. He would treasure the memory of Gisela forever. If the gods granted him someone else to help fill the void left by her departure, he would embrace the gift without regret. In the meantime, he would be thankful for his memories. And try not to lose himself in life at court.

He had no idea how long he stood thus, savoring the tranquillity of the forest. When he reluctantly turned toward home, it was as if he were separated by an invisible shield from the hurly-burly of court life. Without thought he slipped back as silently and unobtrusively as he had left.

When Egar realized he had not been missed, he began to leave the palace at different times of the day and night, striving to do so without being seen. He learned to move slowly but not surreptitiously which in itself drew unwanted attention. He found there was a strong power in his glance. It was natural if he made eye contact with someone, they noticed him in return. To his surprise, he discovered if he so much as let his eyes linger on another's back, they felt the force of the look and turned to him. Egar had to discipline his curious eyes on those occasions when he wanted to leave unnoticed.

The hardest part was the return. He felt so refreshed by his outings away from the claustrophobia of the court that he was hard put to subdue the spring in his step and the sparkle in his eye. With practice he mastered the technique but he could not take away the glow he felt inside.

One afternoon in early summer Egar walked farther than usual into the woods. His busy fingers plucked healing leaves and stems to fill his bag—thyme for lung congestion and coughs, feverfew to treat headache and fever, chamomile to ease an upset stomach.

He was led from sunlight to shadow by the sight of mushrooms. He squatted on the ground, searching his memory for his master's voice and the advice of others since. Some mushrooms were flavorful to eat. Some induced visions. Many were deadly. He chose those he gathered with care.

He paused, estimating the time from the position of the sun's rays as they penetrated the thick forest. It was well on to mid afternoon. How much farther should he go? He must either get back before the main gate at the bridge was closed and bolted or make preparations to spend the night.

The idea of spending the night here—away from the city, the court, people—drew him like a magnet. But where? Not in the open forest. The gods might watch over him, lead him if he were wise enough to follow, but would they save him from a hungry animal if he were stupid enough to put himself in harm's way?

Pushing aside the branches of a giant sycamore, Egar saw a clearing with a small brook. He followed the streamlet until it led him to an outcropping of rock. At the top, a cave looked out on the forest floor. Egar recognized this cave was a place of refuge provided by the gods.

Later that night, sitting before a fire in the mouth of the cave, sated from a supper of fresh fish grilled with mushrooms and a salad of crisp watercress leaves, Egar's thoughts returned to his master and the life they had shared.

The smoke and flame of his small fire twisted and swirled. Gradually they revealed the Old One in his cave. The Master was practicing incantations from an ancient scroll.

Egar knew the Master could not see him, would not hear him.

His thoughts drifted like the smoke. I wonder if he watches me when I am unaware of it? The idea gave him comfort.

What would I say to him? If he could hear me.

Years have come and gone and yet the vision has come no nearer to reality. Except in Pepin's embracement of his role.

What if Pepin is wrong? If the gods do not intend him to be the king, they cannot protect us from our folly in striving to unseat Clothar.

Egar thought once more of Brundhilde's death. If the king would do that to his seventy-year-old aunt, what more would he do to Pepin and me?

With this thought, the image of his Master became clearer. For an instant their eyes locked. Egar read an urgent message of warning in them.

Speak to me, he urged the vision. *Tell me what to do.*

The flame wavered. His master's face dissolved into the smoke.

Chapter Ten

In the spring of 622, Pepin burst into the alcove where Egar was seated at a small table grinding dried seeds of blue creeping gromwell into a powder.

"Your gods have not forgotten us!" Pepin exclaimed. "I will soon have greater influence at court."

Egar stopped his work and gave Pepin his full attention. "What happened?"

"A page summoned me to the king's private chamber. When I arrived Prince Dagobert, Bishop Arnulf and Mayor of the Palace Chucus, were there as well.

"The king announced, 'There is unrest in the kingdom. The nobles of Austrasia, are discontent.'

"Austrasia with its capitol in Metz is the northernmost province of the Franks," Pepin explained. "They feel themselves too far removed from the royal ear, too distant from the seat of power here in Paris."

"What can be done about that?"

"They want a king of their own." Pepin stopped pacing and faced Egar. "I must admit, I thought, if I were king I would march on the nobles with a mighty army. How dare they question the king's authority!

"Fortunately for me I remained silent because Chucus said, 'A number of solutions present themselves. We could march on them with a mighty army. Teach them their place, as it were. But in so doing we would gain their enmity for many generations, to say nothing of the cost to ourselves. Fighting men expect to be paid in gold or lands.'

"So, I thought, what should we do that is better? I admit I might have a thing or two to learn before I will make decisions worthy of the king you saw in your vision."

Egar smiled, glad Pepin strove to merit the crown— whether or not it was his destiny to wear it.

Pepin continued. "Finally, Clothar said, 'We shall agree with our noble subjects. Provide them their heart's desire while yet maintaining control over this most valued area of our realm. We shall give them a king of their own, but one of *our* choosing.'"

"Surely he did not name you?" Egar was incredulous. "It seems too simple."

"No." Pepin smiled. "It will not be *that* simple. Clothar announced he would give them Dagobert as king of Austrasia!"

"Dagobert! But he is only fifteen! And how does this increase your chance to reign?"

"The king acknowledged Dagobert's youth and inexperience. Arnulf is to return to Metz where, in addition to conducting his office as Bishop of Metz, he will act as special advisor to the king. And," Pepin swelled with importance, "*I* am to be sent as Mayor of the Palace!"

"That *is* good news!" Egar grasped Pepin's hand.

He knew his destiny was tied to Pepin's. Somehow he must accompany him to Dagobert's realm.

What a sight the royal procession made as it approached the capital city of Metz! Egar, watching from the side of the road, was hard pressed to contain his excitement. The perfect summer day with its blue sky and warm sun had just a hint of a breeze to furl the banners. Behind him the meadow had sprouted tents like mushrooms after a spring rain. They housed Austrasian noblemen and their retainers from far corners of the province as well as Dagobert's many followers.

The young king led the parade, sitting his white horse proudly. He had not cut his hair since his father gave him reign over Austrasia. The flowing flaxen locks, true mark of Frankish royalty, glowed even brighter than the crown that topped them. He wore a royal purple mantle with golden borders. Though young, he looked every bit the regal monarch.

In places of high honor, Arnulf and Pepin rode just behind their pupil/king. Arnulf, with his usual humility wore the plainest of bishop's robes, but Pepin was adorned in his finest, brightly-colored clothing. A great golden broach clasped his cape at the shoulder.

Behind them a contingent of soldiers shouted from one to the other.

"Today we capture Metz for the young king."

"And after the battle, plunder the countryside as well!"

"Watch out fair maidens!"

They knew their ceremonial silver-hilted swords would remain safely in scabbards. The Merovingian battle standards bearing the blue cloak of Saint Martin fluttered overhead in peace. Their hands would be raised only to drink a toast to the new king.

Horns blew and drums of different sizes and timbres beat exciting tattoos. The sights and sounds made Egar's temples pound as he took his place behind the last of the troops. He was followed by servants and their families who had walked from Paris.

The nobles of Austrasia mounted on their best stallions, formed a corridor through which Dagobert and his court rode. Each nobleman was flanked by foot soldiers holding standards from which flew colorful gonfalons.

"Metz for Dagobert!" rose the cheer.

"Power to Austrasia!"

"Merovingians rule!"

Egar thought they looked pleased with their new king. He guessed they were happy with Dagobert's youth. A sapling is more pliable than an oak, he thought to himself. They can look forward to having their own say in court.

Egar looked in fascination as he passed the massive stone Cathedral of Metz surrounded by its cluster of buildings. The imposing wooden structure next to the cathedral was most likely the bishop's residence. Arnulf would live there and divide his time between cathedral and palace. He saw another large building where he assumed the rest of the monks and brothers slept. Kitchen buildings, work shops and storage sheds made it nearly a city in its own right.

A scattering of tumble-down shacks straggled up the hill to the royal compound. At the open gate of the palace enclosure, Egar was engulfed in a swarm of people, everyone bedecked in his most colorful finery.

"Cheese! Creamy cheese," cried a vendor from behind a huge yellow wheel stacked on a counter.

"Biscuits! Crisp twice-baked biscuits," shouted another.

"Sweet juicy onions!"

"Ale to drink. Dark ale."

Egar was tempted to part with some of his precious coins, but Pepin had promised he could watch the ceremony in which the nobles accepted Dagobert as their king. Besides, if he could but deny his hunger a while longer, there would be feasting in the hall afterwards. Entering the bailey, he savored the aroma of meats roasting over glowing coals as he made his way to the great hall.

Standing at the back, Egar craned his neck trying to see over the crowd. The low hum of conversation filled the air like swarming bees. At last he made his way to the stairs leading to the gallery and chambers above. Leaning over the balustrade, he had a perfect view.

The great hall had been thoroughly swept and aired, the floor laid with fresh rushes. Sunlight flowed through window openings. Walls were decorated with boughs, flowers and banners. Dagobert stood tall, ready to accept the homage of the noblemen and priests who faced him. One by one they knelt, bare headed, swords and axes laid aside.

With his hands between those of Dagobert each noble repeated the oath, "For each and all these lands I make homage and fealty with hands and mouth to thee, my lord, and will defend thee and thy lands against all invaders. So help me God and the saints."

Then Dagobert raised the man to his feet handing him a clod of dirt, symbol of the land over which he had dominion.

A mighty roar sounded as the last of the nobles was sworn. They paraded Dagobert around the hall born aloft on his own shield.

"Hail to our king!"

"Hail Dagobert!"

"Dagobert, King of Austrasia!"

From his perch on the stairs Egar cheered as well.

To Egar it seemed each person knew exactly what his life entailed. Dagobert loved being king—dressing up, playing cards, riding his stallion to the chase. He was charming and gregarious. And seemed to think all lovely young maidens were put in Austrasia for his own personal pleasure.

He cared nothing for the tedious day to day running of the country and was quite content to leave that to Pepin and the others. This suited Pepin well. Noblemen came to him with a complaint or idea and together they arrived at a solution. Wary of powerful, totalitarian monarchists such as Brundhilde had been, they all wanted a strong kingdom with the power in their own hands. When a decision was a *fait accompli* they would present it to the king, who, with all due ceremony ordered it done.

Egar watched as week after week, season following season, ambitious Pepin turned the office of mayor of the palace from a managerial position of running the king's household, into a political power that ran the country. Soon not only the cook and the pages looked to Pepin for direction. Nobles of Austrasia, visiting dignitaries from other Frankish provinces and finally barbarians from beyond the borders and emissaries from Britain, Spain and even Rome sought out Pepin the Vain first, the king second.

Pepin seemed to regarded this as perfect training for his promised destiny, to be king of all Franks.

Take care, Pepin! Egar felt like shouting out. *The vision was not so clear as you want to make it.*

But was he responsible for Pepin's obsession for the throne? Egar had never promised it would be his. And Pepin no doubt understood the danger even better than he.

Even Grimwald, ten years old at the coronation, knew what was expected of him. He and Ansegisel, Bishop Arnulf's son from a marriage before he entered the religious life, were inseparable. Indeed Ansegisel spent far more time in Pepin's household than he did in the bishop's residence. Each morning the boys ran, laughing and tussling like puppies, to classes within the cathedral compound. Afternoons were spent in soldiers' training on the palace grounds.

At last, Egar found a niche for himself. It had nothing to do with his long-promised destiny, but it did give him a role in the life of Metz.

An old woman who was skilled in concocting remedies welcomed Egar into her solitary home. They worked companionably together and he learned new ways of healing from her.

Old and feeble, she sat on her stool by the fire and directed Egar. "See you that shapeless bunch of dried weeds that be hanging there?"

At his answering nod, she continued, "That be yarrow. Use it to stanch a wound. And this shepherd's purse be curing flux of the bowels."

At last, one frigid winter's day Egar found a cold and lifeless body wrapped in a fur coverlet. She had died peacefully in her sleep.

No one came to claim the old woman's hut and the peasants who arrived there for cures seemed to take it for granted that Egar would be available to help them. He came to spend more and more time there, eventually taking it over as living accommodations and healer's dispensary.

He was relieved to have time and space to himself away from the crowded quarters of the palace. Here he would make a small fire in the table brazier and sit staring into it by the hour. Occasionally he caught a glimpse of his beloved Old Master in the smoke and flame. No sound. No communication between them. It was nonetheless comforting to Egar to know he was still in the cave on the hill.

As he had in Paris, Egar roamed the forests surrounding Metz, searching for healing herbs and remedies. He never entered the forest without missing Gisela. He wished her well fulfilling her destiny as a priestess, but longed for the flesh and blood relationship they had briefly shared so many years ago.

The years passed. Pepin grew older, weighted no doubt by responsibility. Dagobert became nearly a contemporary. Egar, alas, felt himself neither increase in age nor mature in wisdom.

Chapter Eleven

One day, nearly three years after Dagobert's coronation, a messenger arrived from Clothar informing the court at Metz to expect the king in a fortnight's time. The city was abuzz. The great hall was prepared for Clothar's visit. Everyone, from Dagobert and Pepin down to the smallest swine-herd conjectured as to the meaning of this royal sojourn.

Dagobert, wearing a blue and gold mantle over his shirt of finest linen, went out into the yard to meet his father. He was surrounded by noblemen dressed in their brightest colors with arm bracelets and broaches aplenty. His royal guard stood at attention, their pennants and ganfalons undulating in the breeze.

Looking around at those who had come to welcome his father, Dagobert thought, Clothar may rule Neustria and Burgundy, but *I* am king here. His chest swelled, pride pushing aside curiosity.

Clothar arrived, his stallion glittering with silver tack. Six of his royal mounted guard followed. Dagobert was stunned to see his father's long hair showing strands of grey.

Ignoring the noblemen and guards, Clothar led Dagobert followed by Pepin and Arnulf to the royal living quarters. With just the four of them around a table, it seemed like old times in Paris.

After a long draught of thirst-quenching ale, Clothar cleared his throat. "Dagobert, it is time you were wed."

Dagobert should not have been surprised by the statement. He was of age for marriage. Mating and siring sons was a major requirement for the monarchy. But it was, nevertheless, the furthest thing from his mind.

"I have made inquiries," his father continued, "and found a bride for you. She comes from a noble family, of course. Her father, Widukind, has vast estates on the northern border. A strong alliance with him will be militarily advantageous when the Saxons try, as they will again, to invade our territories. Her dowry is excellent. A dozen stallions, gold and jewels, as well as household items and attendants.

"Her name is Gomatrud and she is said to be young and comely. But then every daughter is beautiful in her father's eyes. We shall have to wait and see on that."

Dagobert sat, stunned. "You have already found her? But, when will it... will I..."

"The banns will be posted Sunday. Arnulf, take care of it."

Arnulf bowed in acknowledgement.

"The wedding will take place in about two months time, near Midsummer Day. Gomatrud, her father, her household and dowry will arrive a few days prior."

Dagobert's head swirled. No one asked him whether these plans met with his approval. He understood neither the bride nor he had any say in the matter. And yet...

* * *

Gomatrud arrived at Metz bringing with her, besides her father and the stallions, a full retinue of pages and ladies-in-waiting. A train of wagons pulled by oxen and loaded high with household items followed. One could glimpse a bed frame, several huge carved chests, large and small looms, as well as pots and kettles of all sizes.

Her party rode through an encampment of tents ablaze with banners. It seemed everyone in the kingdom had come to witness the wedding.

When Dagobert rode out to meet the princess he was pleased to find she was indeed young and very beautiful. She wore a simple white dress with embroidered waist of gold and jewels and was mounted on a palfrey the color of fresh cream, her father by her side. Her hair was a halo of spun gold about her fair face. Her guard wore tunics and short capes in the family colors of forest green and brown.

People cheered.

Dagobert knew they would make a magnificent couple, both of them fine-featured and fair. Smiling in relief, he brought his stallion around to ride side by side with his betrothed through the crowd and into the town of Metz where boxes of flowers bloomed at every window.

The day dawned clear and bright. For a moment when Gomatrud opened her eyes, she could not remember where she was. With a shiver, realization dawned. She hugged herself to contain feelings that threatened to overflow. Let loose they would cause her to dance and laugh and weep—all at the same time. Today she was to wed!

Like every young girl, she had long dreamed of this day—wearing a beautiful gown, being handed by her father to a handsome young prince, living happily ever after. But now the fateful day had arrived, she was filled with apprehension. How far distant from the dream would reality prove to be?

She had confessed her fears to the strange priest in the large cathedral, but he said such anxiety was normal. He admonished her to do what was expected of her by both God and her father—be a dutiful and obedient daughter, bride and wife.

Ladies-in-waiting helped her put on fine undergarments, painstakingly embroidered with flowers, birds and other symbols of fertility. She was shaking by the time they carefully pulled the wedding dress fashioned from silk richly adorned with brocade, lace and pearls, over her head. Her hair was carefully dressed. A veil shrouded both it and her blushing face.

A crowd filled the cathedral for early morning Mass proceeding the wedding ceremony. Gomatrud, with her father and ladies-in-waiting, stood in an alcove to the side of the huge central chamber. As people in the congregation turned to stare at her, she was thankful to hide behind the veil.

At last she raised her eyes to glimpse at Dagobert. Seated on a raised dais at the front of the church, he was resplendent in a fine white tunic trimmed in gold. A royal purple cloak draped his shoulders and a gold coronet encircled his head. Her heart thumped. How handsome he was! She hardly noticed King Clothar and Pepin standing close by.

The Mass finally began. Gomatrud was comforted to realize that, although the building and people were foreign to her, the service itself was blessedly familiar. Candles burned brightly as the monks sang the Gregorian chant opening the liturgy. An acolyte entered swinging the censer. The smell of beeswax was overcome by the sweet fragrance of incense. Gomatrud knelt with the rest as bishop Arnulf began.

She felt the nervous fluttering in her empty stomach quiet as the Mass continued with words from the bishop, well known responses murmured by the congregation, and the chant floating softly from the choir loft. By the time Arnulf spoke the words dismissing the worshipers, she was surprised to find she was quite calm.

The wedding party proceeded to the rail for the simple ceremony. Gomatrud fingered the cross on its heavy golden chain. It had been in her family for generations.

Arnulf asked, "Who gives this woman to be married?" and her father, with a last loving look, handed her to Dagobert. A heavy gold ring carved with a replica of the Merovingian crest was blessed by the priest and then slipped onto the bride's finger. Much too large for her to wear, it would soon find its way next to the cross on the chain around her neck.

When Arnulf asked if she would honor and obey Dagobert she answered "I will," with hardly a qualm.

Gomatrud felt a wave of loneliness as they were declared "man and wife". Soon her father and most of the servants would depart and she would be left with strangers.

She watched in fascination as the witnesses signed their names and the date in a large book. She was properly impressed by the squiggles and scratches that recorded her union for all to see.

Chapter Twelve

The wedding party entered the Great Hall where countless noblemen and their families waited to greet Gomatrud and Dagobert personally. Fortunately she and her new subjects spoke the same language. She could manage, barely, in Latin but the Teutonic tongue and life-style were familiar to her. She felt welcome in her new home, able to converse with those who would become her family.

The nuptial gifts were piled at the foot of the raised dais in a display of jewels, laces, and hand embroidery. A baldric—the strap from which Dagobert would hang his sword—flashed with gold and precious stones. The gift of two puppies sired by a famous hunting hound were immediately removed from the hall by a page.

Gomatrud was exhausted and feeling faint from hunger, excitement, or having stood too long. She and Dagobert were finally seated in their beautifully carved chairs. The nobles, equally thankful, seated themselves on benches at long trestle tables.

Gomatrud looked about the great hall, so much larger than her father's. She could hardly believe she was now queen of the realm and would live in this palace forever. The walls were colorful with banners bearing the Merovingian insignia as well as those of visiting nobles. Her eyes lingered on the beloved stag's head denoting her own family. It would remain here, proclaiming the queen's lineage to all who entered.

She glanced shyly at her husband and felt a dreamy wonderment fill her heart. Her belongings would by now have been moved to the queen's quarters, immediately next to his. Tonight we will lie touching each other in the same bed. Our marriage will be consummated. She was not entirely ignorant of what this entailed. She had witnessed the mating and birth of animals, but this was different. Would he be gentle? Would it hurt? She had heard so many conflicting tales she knew not whether to anticipate the event with excitement or dread.

Delicious aromas put an end to her wandering thoughts. Pages staggered in under huge platters, a whole roast pig, pies containing birds of every size and description, breads and cheeses, onions and cabbages. Proudly the pages marched around the hall showing all assembled the quantity and variety of foods with which the court celebrated the wedding of its king and queen.

Kegs of ale flowed as well as wine, spiced and heated, served in great goblets.

At the same time the entire peasant population of Metz was feasting out of doors, as guests of the crown, on meats cooked over open spits, great cheeses and sweetmeats.

After the feast cries went out.

"Egar, we would be entertained."

"What have you in your bag of tricks?"

Gomatrud watched in fascination as the one named Egar took a fistful of black powder and flung it to the floor with considerable force. The powder exploded unexpectedly in a roar and puff of smoke. She screamed and jumped—as did everyone in the hall. When the concealing smoke cleared, Egar emerged, draped from shoulders to floor in a black cape covered in mystic symbols embroidered in thread of gold.

"Ahhh." Murmurs of appreciation filled the silence.

Ceremoniously, Egar tossed the flowing cape behind him. He held out his hand. It held a brightly colored orange ball. With a toss of his hand the orange disappeared. Two smaller balls, one green, one purple took its place. He closed his fist. Then flung up, not one, not two, but three balls, each bigger than the one before. Bright red, blue, and yellow. Without so much as a pause he was juggling seven balls in the air at the same time.

The crowd stamped and cheered, banging their tankards on the trestle tables in approval.

The balls suddenly disappeared as mysteriously as they had materialized. Egar's hands were empty. A hush fell over the great hall. Suddenly everyone looked at Gomatrud. All of the balls, in bright colors and various sizes had magically appeared on the table before her!

"A small wedding gift, my lady, queen," bowed Egar. "Something for you to play with when you will."

She smiled in delight. Surely, life in this wondrous kingdom would not be so terrifying with subjects such as this winsome young magician to entertain. She hoped he was not an itinerant traveling performer whom she might never see again.

Dagobert, lounging beside his young bride, was completely captivated by her beauty. Despite the feasting and revelry going on all around them, he found it hard to take his eyes off this dainty maiden. None of the compliant young women he had bedded thus far could compare in looks to his lovely young wife.

We will make a perfect pair, Dagobert thought, and produce wonderful royal progeny. He was anxious to begin.

The room buzzed with expectation as Egar brought forth his large court harp. He seated himself and stroked a chord. With the sound the room became silent.

"I sing in celebration of the wedding of our beloved king and queen," Egar began, "but 'Dagobert's Song' begins, not here and now, but rightly commences many years ago with Meroveus, the first of the Merovingians."

A second silvery chord floated from Egar's harp. The torches, snuffed by an errant gust of wind, left the hall in flickering, smoky shadows.

A third chord whispered over the shadows, and the great hall itself disappeared into a grey mist.

Egar sang. Clodio took a summer bath in the sea, his wife nearby. Suddenly Clodio disappeared into the foamy water. As he sank beneath the surface he was transformed and in his place, out of the depths of the ocean rose a mighty, scaly sea-beast. His nostrils belched smoke, eyes flashed shafts of fire. The huge reptile approached Clodio's fair wife seated upon the sand. She feared him not and of this mating of serpent and maiden was born Meroveus, progenitor of the Merovingians.

> *And he was born of a sea-beast,*
> *of a serpent was he born,*
> *Proud Merovingians born of the sea-beast,*
> *serpent of the deep brings them the crown.*

Egar sang of Clovis I, King of All Franks. In 496, after a prayer for assistance to his wife's God, Clovis won a stunning victory over the Allemans. He, along with three thousand of his soldiers, immediately converted to Christianity.

> *And he was born of a sea-beast,*
> *of a serpent was he born ...*

Egar sang of Fredegund and Brunhilde, of Clothar II and of Dagobert.

> *...serpent of the deep brings them the crown.*

* * *

Torches flickered then burned more brightly. The great hall emerged once again. Stunned silence greeted the song. Egar's music was as filled with magic as was his sleight of hand.

Everyone began talking at once. Egar, as his wedding gift to the royal couple, had created for them a legendary beginning. Perhaps, the wedding guests murmured, this is why only those with Merovingian blood can reign. Because only they are descended from a sea-serpent.

In that instant the legend became history. The court and wedding guests cheered the song and Egar, creator of the saga. Finally they stood as one, facing their king and queen, pledging their hearts as well as their homage.

Later that evening, Egar was startled when Pepin burst furiously into his alcove.

"How could you!" Pepin sputtered. "How could you sing thus of Dagobert and the Merovingians? I thought you were my ally. I believed when you said I would be king. But now you make heroes of the Merovingians. After this night their fame will be sung by every singer in the kingdom.

"I have no chance of becoming king now. Everyone knows the serpent always wins. I am lost before I begin. And the fault is yours. Yours and that vicious song you made."

"It was only my wedding gift to a man who has been my friend as well as my king," argued Egar. "I need not 'take sides' against him for you. I am on the side of the gods and the destiny they plan will happen—song or no."

Egar stopped as a preposterous idea sprang into his head. Could a song—merely the singer's attempt to entertain—be taken for the stuff of legend? *Britain's legend has come and gone but it will live on in poetry and song.* The priest's voice rang in Egar's head.

"I doubt not the vision was a true one," he said quietly, breaking the silence. "When the destiny is achieved, then will I sing 'Pepin's Song' and it will spread the fame of the greatest king of all time. It will live in history from the day it is sung to the edges of human memory."

Pepin felt Egar's words beckoning him into an unimaginable future. "You will have some task to surpass the song you gave Dagobert this day. But I doubt not you can do it if you set your heart to the matter."

"Whether or not you are he who will be king," Egar whispered, "your fame will live. Your might will overcome those descended of the sea-beast. You and the family that flows from your loins will be celebrated in poetry and lays long after the Merovingians are forgotten."

When Egar turned, his countenance reflected a radiance far beyond the feeble light of the torch. His eyes were focused on some vision beyond the confines of the alcove.

Pepin's heart hammered with expectation. Egar's words drove him to new heights of aspiration. He would be that king. It was ordained.

In the climaxing event of those halcyon years in Metz, Queen Gomatrud was delivered of a healthy male son and heir. He was baptized Sigibert III.

The kingdom rejoiced in his birth. Masses were celebrated, toasts drunk, "To the prince. Long live the Merovingian prince!"

The throne was assured.

Not even the birth of Sigibert could disturb Pepin's calm. He remained aloof and optimistic. Egar's words the night of the royal wedding still rang in his ears. He would be king, male heir or not. It was written in the stars and only the hand of God could do that.

* * *

In 629, King Clothar II died. Dagobert I became king, not only of his own Austrasian realm, but King of All Franks, those in Neustria and Burgundy as well.

The gods gave Egar no sign, no premonition, that with the old king's death the entire realm would become like a fresh egg with a cracked shell. It did not occur to him that no one, not Dagobert, not Arnulf, not even Pepin, would be able to put it together again.

Chapter Thirteen

Egar rode near the back of the royal procession returning from Paris and Clothar's funeral. The sky was leaden and a chill rain fell. The bare trees of the forest emerged from tendrils of fog like black-boned skeletons. No one spoke. Each man hunkered down into himself to escape the cold and to brood.

Egar realized there were bound to be changes at court now that Dagobert had inherited his father's realm. He wondered in what way Clothar's death would aid or thwart the god's plans and his place in them.

Once returned to Metz, Dagobert called a meeting of the bishops and antrustions of Austrasia who made up his council. Pennants and banners in the great hall were draped with black denoting a household in deep mourning and everyone wore clothing of unusually somber colors. Dagobert sat on the raised dais, his only ornament a plain golden crown. He watched as the council arranged themselves by rank at the trestle table below.

Acknowledging their expressions of sympathy, Dagobert announced, "As you all know, with my father's death, I have inherited the realms of Neustria and Burgundy as well as our Austrasia. After considerable thought, I have decided I must move my court.

"While my heart will always carry a special love for Metz and the Austrasian kingdom, I and the court will in the future reside in Paris."

"But you are *our* king!"

"We *need* you here!"

"What will we do with you gone?"

Dagobert was amused by their clamor. He would not, however, change his mind. "I am not needed here. Pepin will remain in Metz. With him at your head you have been making most of the decisions all along."

I resent the ease with which Pepin has prevailed, Dagobert thought. It is only because I was so young when I became king that he has been allowed to do so. But now I shall return to Paris without proud Pepin at my heels. He forgets he is no longer the tutor and I the childish pupil!

"Continue to administer Austrasia as you have," he told the council. "When you need me, Paris is no farther away than it ever was. You will always be welcome at our court there. You of Austrasia will always have our ear."

"My lord, king," replied Pepin, "we shall miss your shining presence in our midst but we will do our utmost to see that Austrasia continues to give you glory and riches."

Dagobert could not miss the relish with which Pepin as mayor of the palace, looked forward to being the sole authority in Metz.

Egar wondered whether he would be expected to return to Paris or allowed to remain in Metz with Pepin. Although his vision had tied him to Pepin, he remained at the king's pleasure.

"What should I do?" he asked Pepin when they were alone.

"Do you wish to stay?"

"I shall miss Dagobert," replied Egar. "But my destiny is joined to yours. I would be with you, if allowed."

"Leave it to me. After all, Paris will have its own exciting new diversions for the king and queen."

Everyone in Metz was pressed into service to prepare for the king's move. Even Grimwald and Ansegisel helped by climbing up to take down the banners and pennants lining the great hall.

"Take care with those now," cried the head chambermaid. "By my faith, see how dusty and dirty they have become hanging in all that smoke."

Many hands helped carry them outside where they were aired and then packed away.

The armorer and the local blacksmith were busy from sun-up to dark cleaning and repairing swords and shields as they were taken off the walls. The constant hammering made Egar's head ache and filled him with a hollow feeling of forboding.

With Pepin at his side, Dagobert sorted through the treasure. The glow of jewels and gold filled him with pleasure.

"But surely, sire," protested Pepin, "you will not take *all* of this to Paris with you?"

Dagobert polished a coin with his thumb. "I shall leave a small portion here. But I must take most of it. Once in Paris, who knows what expenses I shall face?"

And, he thought to himself, it will do you good to have to cut back on your expenses, my vain advisor. By controlling the purse strings, I shall rein your ambition.

The whole town turned out to bid farewell to their king and queen. Many of their friends and neighbors—guards, pages, ladies-in-waiting, cooks, grooms, clerks, scribes, and their households were leaving as well. Women waved handkerchiefs. Men shouted oaths and advice. Dogs barked, chasing among the horses' hooves. Children, giddy with excitement, screamed and shouted, getting in everyone's way.

Royal guards in leather tunics patrolled, both for protection and to maintain an orderly line of march. Dagobert rode his white horse while Gomatrud and her lady-in-waiting with baby Sigibert and his nurse rode in litters near the head. They were followed by royal wagons filled to overflowing with imperial possessions.

After them came every kind of conveyance piled high with more homely objects. Many had baskets of geese and chickens next to where small children perched among the feather quilts. If the family was more fortunate than most, a sow might be heard squealing in protest or a cow seen plodding along behind. Many would walk the whole way from Metz to Paris next to the cart bearing all their worldly possessions.

Abruptly the last of those moving were gone. Suddenly it was too quiet. When all that could be seen of the court was a pall of dust smudging the horizon, those remaining sighed and returned to home, field or shop. Pepin walked alone into the great hall. It was silent and empty. Dust motes hung lazily in the still air.

Arnulf, Bishop of Metz, sighed, at the sound of his prior's discreet clearing of the throat. He closed his Bible, crossed himself before the crucifix on the wall, then stood.

"Forgive me, Father," the prior said, "for interrupting your devotions. But the cellarer reports the supply of seeds for spring planting is less than it should be. The sacrist requests a new book as ours has pages that are torn and missing. And the novice master says he must speak with you, personally."

Not for the first time, Arnulf longed for that earlier time in his life when he had been excused from King Clothar's service to enter a monastery and become a monk. His thoughts flew backward. At that time, his wife, Clothar's cousin, Blithilda, had decided to become a nun—with the blessings of both Clothar and Arnulf, himself. Their infant son, Ansegisel, was cared for by nursemaids of the court. The realm was at peace and Arnulf was allowed at last to fulfill his calling.

The peace was short lived, and so was Arnulf's career as monk.

"Thank you, Prior John." Arnulf returned once more to the present. "I shall see to the novice master. I doubt more seed is likely to be had. Best we tend what we have with careful hands and prayerful hearts. Tell the sacrist to send to the scriptorium in Paris for the necessary replacement pages. We cannot, in good conscience, request a whole new book."

Arnulf took another deep breath as the prior nodded, turned and left. His eyes swept the austere sitting room. Bare whitewashed walls relieved only by the large crucifix at one end. Small brazier of glowing coals on a table in front of which stood a high-backed chair, benches on either side. In one corner a large table covered in books, scrolls, writing tablets, stylus, pen, ink. I could, he thought fondly, exchange this for a cell in a monastery without a pang of regret.

With a rush of buoyancy, he thought, why not?

A few weeks later, Arnulf sought Pepin. He found the mayor of the palace sitting at the cluttered table in his living quarters. "Do you have a few minutes for an old friend?"

Pepin looked up, an expression of pleasure on his face. "Of course. For you, anything."

"You know I have long wished for the contemplative life." At Pepin's slight frown, Arnulf continued quickly. "My obligation to the crown ended with Clothar's death. Dagobert has agreed to appoint a younger man bishop and given me permission to return to the monastery."

"I will sorely miss your friendship. Especially now." Pepin rubbed his temple as though his head had started to ache. "I thought when the king moved it would be as though he were merely out hunting. I had no idea that with him would go more than half of Metz."

Arnulf felt a tug of sadness. Although several years Pepin's senior, they had begun serving the Merovingian monarchy together under Brundhilde and her son Theudebert II. They had left the ill-fated queen to serve her nephew, Clothar, when the old lady's dictatorial ways had become too much to bear. But Clothar was dead. Arnulf was free to follow his heart.

"I value your companionship. But I miss time to meditate even more. I juggle responsibilities the way Egar juggles balls. While working at one task, I think about six others."

Pepin smiled and nodded his understanding.

"I need to focus on what is truly important," Arnulf continued. "I tire of continually making requests of Christ. I would devote myself to His message for us instead. My soul hungers for quiet."

"I am selfish," answered Pepin. "I would keep you with me forever if I could."

"There is one thing. Before I renounce the world I would see my son, Ansegisel, and your daughter, Bega, betrothed—if you approve."

"Nothing would please me more. Itta and I already look upon Ansegisel as a son." Pepin sat in silence, his chin resting on his fingers. At last he spoke. "Bega is but eleven. I hesitate to see her wed for another year or two."

"They are both young. Assured of the betrothal, I need not witness the nuptials. Ansegisel would be honored to marry Bega. What male in his right mind would not! But I would have Bega pleased, as well."

More than pleased, Bega was delighted. For years she had idolized both her older brother and his friend, Ansegisel. Her only complaint was in having to wait.

Chapter Fourteen

What members of the court remained, dined in the great hall for the main meal of the day. With the departure of the king and queen, their ranks had shrunk. Pepin's family, Arnulf, who frequently dined there with Ansegisel, Egar, craftsmen and a captain of the guard or two and their families filled but two or three trestle tables. Visiting nobles were a rarity.

When all had finished eating, Pepin stood. "As her father, it is my very pleasant duty to announce the betrothal of my daughter, Bega, to Ansegisel, son of Bishop Arnulf."

"Three cheers for Bega and Ansegisel!" shouted the guardsmen, doing their best to fill the empty corners of the huge room with sound.

"Ansegisel will truly be my brother at last!" cried Grimwald.

"Stand up, you two," ordered Pepin.

Bega and Ansegisel, blushing, stood joining hands.

"I have long thought of you as a daughter," said Arnulf. "I am pleased you will truly be so. Take good care of her, my son."

The three of them embraced.

"Come round the table," shouted the guards. "We have words for you."

"Put a board between you during the waiting time from betrothal to wedding else it be a fat bride that goes to the chapel," advised a captain to good humored laughter.

"Ho, blacksmith, devise a chastity belt and throw away the key," cried another.

The young couple blushed even deeper as they, too, laughed at the teasing.

Every man in Metz envied Ansegisel. Bega, beautiful and charming, stood on the threshold of maidenhood. She had Itta's fine features, creamy complexion, and dark hair, but Pepin's brilliant blue eyes and enthusiastic love of life.

Ansegisel was a good match. Slender, tall—and serious, as would be expected from Arnulf's son. But he laughed more than his father, perhaps because he had been raised almost as one of Pepin's own.

Grimwald and Ansegisel clasped forearms in a strong grip of friendship. "Watch out for that little she-child," said Grimwald of his sister, "else she beat you up. She is stronger than she looks and will run you a merry chase."

Ansegisel made as if to defend his beloved's honor and the two of them ended in a tussle that belied their years.

In contrast to the court's move, Arnulf's packing took less than an hour. He folded two shirts, one cloak, three pair of stockings, an extra pair of drawers, two leggings, his wooden shoes, and a pair of sandals. Reverently he kissed and carefully wrapped his most prized possessions, his Bible and his crucifix. All his worldly possessions fit easily into two saddlebags.

He intended to make the four or five day trip by himself but Ansegisel would hear none of it. He could not forego a last opportunity to share his father's company. When Grimwald heard of the journey, he too, insisted on going. After all, he could keep Ansegisel company on the return trip. Grimwald asked Pepin's permission. Pepin readily agreed and decided to go along as well.

Bega used every one of her formidable feminine wiles to be allowed to join them. Pepin could see no harm in it but Itta refused to allow her to go in a party comprised exclusively of males. In the end there was nothing for it but to have Itta ride with them, much to Bega's delight. Egar caught word of the journey and was granted permission to join the group.

They traveled with a minimum of men and baggage. Itta was carried in a litter but Bega enjoyed riding her small palfrey with the men. Porters led pack mules loaded with food, tents, blankets and rugs. They followed the Moselle River, eating and sleeping out of doors, enjoying the gentle spring sun.

Ansegisel drew next to his father, the rest of the group strung out along the shaded pathway. "I want you to know I am happy for you, but..."

"But?" urged Arnulf.

At the extended silence Arnulf finished his son's thought. "But you are angry I am leaving."

"It hurts to think you would choose a monastery closed to the world, over watching me marry and father your grandchildren."

"I do love you," protested Arnulf.

"I know, but only as you love all people, as a priest, not a father."

"I love you the only way I know. Because I have a calling, think not I love you less when I must serve Our Lord."

"I wish you well and hope you will think of me—of us." Ansegisel looked lovingly at Bega.

Arnulf recognized Ansegisel's hurt. He leaned over and gripped his son's shoulder. "You will remain in my heart, thoughts and prayers, my dear son." There was nothing he could do to ease the pain he was causing.

Pepin took the place next to Arnulf as Ansegisel with a sad smile, urged his horse forward to join Bega.

"I do not understand this desire you have to leave the exciting challenges of the real world to molder away in some isolated abbey, pondering imponderables."

"I know. It is much easier to accept your desire for the throne," said Arnulf good-naturedly, "than it is to comprehend my choice as a monk."

At the word 'throne' Pepin looked quickly around.

"Look not so startled." Arnulf smiled. "Your ambition is well known. We would all have to be both deaf and blind not to see you fancy yourself king and far superior to him who now reigns. As long as you are not so foolish as to act upon that wish, no harm done."

Pepin's glance went to Egar. Arnulf saw the look and pondered its meaning. Just who was this likeable young pagan magician and what ideas had he put into Pepin's head?

The rest of the afternoon Arnulf and Pepin rode together remembering times shared. They laughed over experiences that were amusing only in retrospect. Priest and soldier, they had fought many battles side by side.

Arnulf chose the abbey at Remiremont as his place of retreat. He said farewell to each of them in turn, admonishing Bega and Ansegisel to love and protect each other, giving a small book of prayers to Itta as thanks for the mothering she had given both his future daughter-in-law and his own son.

Pepin and he embraced. They could not speak their thoughts; emotions were too near the surface.

At last he and Egar stood facing each other. Arnulf's eyes bored into Egar who tried unsuccessfully to summon power to send the look back. Egar broke the gaze first, staring down at his feet.

"I know not who you are or what hold you have on Pepin," said Arnulf quietly, "but if you value your soul, do nothing that will cause him harm."

Egar's head snapped and he looked at Arnulf with wide eyes. "I would not cause him pain. I love him as mentor and friend. If there be pain, it is the result of the gods' own gifts."

At last, with promises to remember each other in their prayers, the party painfully separated at the abbey's gates.

The effect of the royal relocation was far-reaching. Metz consisted of a collection of huts clustered around the palace grounds. The removal of so many people seriously threatened the stability of the town.

As spring turned to summer, tradesmen and their families headed for Paris, Soissons, or other cities offering greater opportunity. Farmers found it difficult to sell their products on market days. Nobles with estates had left long since to see to their own lands. Those who served at the king's pleasure went with him to Paris to further their fortunes.

That year, on midsummer's eve, Egar went to a clearing in the forest. He stood watch, as once he had stood at Stonehenge, hoping to gain reassurance from the gods that his destiny still awaited him. As darkness fell he became aware of the hoot of an owl, the soft movement of air as a bat brushed by in flight. His legs grew numb as he watched the stars move almost imperceptibly across the vast heavens.

With all his heart Egar wanted to see the constellations begin to swirl and dance to unheard celestial music. He wanted to feel connected as if the entire universe were a harp and he but one of its strings. To feel himself tremble and hum as if *he* were being plucked by the gods. But as the stars continued to wheel slowly on their assigned paths he remained unmoved. The night seemed silent and coldly out of reach.

The sky lightened in the east and he beheld the first piercing ray of sunlight. Egar felt tired, his eyes burning and gritty from lack of sleep. Gone was the exhilaration he had felt standing with the priests of Stonehenge. Although he knew this first shaft of sun had once again found its way straight through the opening of the standing stones to illuminate the altar inside, the thought seemed unreal to him. It had no connection with his own life.

Egar wondered if he had angered the gods, causing them to turn their backs. Then with a sigh and shake of his head he thought it more likely that he and his destiny were of such insignificance the gods had simply forgotten him.

As summer faded into fall, Metz, once rich and bustling became a ghost of its former self. Buildings left uninhabited became derelict. It felt as if a rushing river had changed course, leaving in its wake, a shallow, algae-filled puddle.

Winter was especially hard that year. The cold and snow accentuated their isolation. The court in Paris was far, far away.

Pepin was determined to pull the town out of its decline come spring. Then people would recognize his right to be king and would demand he be so appointed.

Snow piled high against the palisade wall. Wind whistled through cracks in the shutters. Pepin realized he had not seen Egar in several days.

He sent a guard to check. Egar was nowhere to be found.

Chapter Fifteen

The snow slowly gave way to Spring of 630. The great hall reeked with winter odors of smoke and unwashed bodies.

One day, Pepin, hearing his name, came out on the gallery and looked down. Below him, two guards staggered in, leaving the door open to gusts of frigid air. They supported Egar between them. Pepin leaped down the stairs only to pull short at the sight of the young magician.

Egar looked and smelled as if he had spent the winter in a cave with a hibernating bear. His hair was wild and grown well past his shoulders. His eyes, sunk deep into shadowed sockets, held a haunted quality. He had aged. His sunken cheeks were covered by a matted beard.

"Egar, by my faith!" exclaimed Pepin. "What in the name of all that is holy happened to you? Where have you been?"

Egar opened his mouth. He swayed and would have fallen had not the two guards caught him. Carefully they half carried Egar to his pallet in the alcove.

"Wish you our help with him?" they asked.

"No. We can manage." Pepin turned to a page watching with eyes wide and mouth agape. "Run. Fetch Lady Itta."

"Yes, my lord!"

"Where did you find him?" Pepin asked of the guards.

"Outside the palace gate. He was delirious."

"You did well to bring him. My wife knows something of the healing arts. God grant Egar will respond to her care."

"Egar is a favorite," said a guard. "We wish him well."

They saluted Itta who hurried in followed by the page.

She helped Pepin peal off Egar's grimy, stinking clothes. She handed the putrid rags to the page. "Tell a servant to burn them. And run to cook in the kitchen. We need a large basin of warm water."

She washed Egar's body. He was unaware of her kind attentions. Although clearly starved and feverish as well, he seemed not to be wounded. Itta tried to feed him but he could not be roused enough to sip the broth she offered.

Egar slept through the entire day and night, his breathing steady though labored. His eyes fluttered open late the next afternoon. He looked at Itta and Pepin without recognition, but was able to swallow a little broth before falling into a deep sleep. The next morning he awoke with clear eyes. Though frightfully weak, he knew who and where he was.

"Where did you go? What happened to you?" queried Pepin.

"The forest." Egar shivered. He could say no more.

How could he explain to them the nightmare he had endured in that dark and wild place—make them understand why he had gone there at all?"

Egar had grown progressively more despondent and unsettled as the past summer faded into fall. While

Pepin was as determined to rule as ever, Egar had no inkling as to his own role. The gods sent him no messages, save that one long-ago vision of the great king.

He sought reassurance his god-given destiny still awaited him. While gathering healing herbs in the forests surrounding Metz, he pondered the old gods where he found them still with power—in stone cairns, a hollowed giant tree trunk, or the crystal of a spring. His life depended on their direction but they gave no hint he had ever played a part in their grand design for the universe.

Egar became increasingly aware of areas in the deep forest where evil dwelt. In a black marsh, skeletal trees stretched ghostly bare branches above stagnant waters and ethereal blue flames danced. Below the surface lived demons ready to grasp any living thing that dared walk there, dragging it downward until it disappeared forever.

Nearby was a small space in the middle of a dense grove where branches grew so thickly overhead, daylight never penetrated. There a lamia, a female demon, grew strong on the blood of human sacrifices. Her temple was a large outcropping of obsidian, carved with unreadable symbols.

Egar was as curious about the power of evil as he was of that of the more familiar gods. Little by little he dared go closer. One moonless winter's night he followed the sound of chanting deeper into the forest than he had ever gone before. As he watched he saw barely visible shapes moving, flitting, drawing him onward. Suddenly he felt a chill creep down his spine, as if the frozen wings of a giant vulture folded silently around his body.

Egar smelt death. Turning to flee, he found he was surrounded by every demon in the murky realm. He felt like an animal at bay. No matter where he turned they were snapping at his heels. He protected his body as long as he was able. Fended them off with his sword, thrown stones, a branch, his knife—his bare hands. There were too many of them. At last he could hold them off no longer.

The evil spirits invaded his skin, exerting excruciating pain. Each seemed armed with sharp knives and burning coals. Egar's every joint—knees, fingers, elbows—felt as if they were being broken, slowly so as to extend the agony. A hot coal was forced into his mouth. Cruelly, it burned the soft tissues of tongue, cheeks and gums. He could neither swallow nor spit it out. At one point his internal organs seemed to be ripped from his body. Where his stomach and entrails had been was put a living demon armed with sharp teeth which it used with horrible effect.

While surrendering his body, piece by piece, Egar tried with every skill and power of thought he had, to save his mind. He gathered his diminishing resources around it, as one might build a palisade around a palace keep. One by one his powers of concentration became too weak, too distracted by pain, to serve his mind. Finally, in desperation he flung his thoughts as high into the heavens as he was able, focusing on the stars that had wheeled above Stonehenge on that first, dimly remembered midsummer's eve.

With that mighty effort he found he no longer had to think, make decisions. All that was left was to endure the torture and survive.

Egar knew intuitively all the trials would stop if he agreed to serve the evil ones. It would be so easy to offer his god-given destiny to serve a dark and sinister plan. But this he could not do. He could give up his body, send his mind to some untouchable plain, but he could not offer his life to promote harm and suffering.

Egar had no idea how long he remained in the overwhelming power of evil. Time had no meaning. At last, as he was about to surrender to the lure of death, he became aware of a far-off light offering solace and reprieve.

Fearfully, Egar opened his eyes and saw Gisela standing alone in the forest. The light he had seen radiated from her as if it were a protective shield. Long blond hair gently framed her face. Blue eyes spoke silently of love. She wore the flowing white robe of a priestess.

As he reached out to her she said wordlessly, "No, my love, you must not touch me. But rest now. I am here to guard you. You are safe. Their evil is no match for our gods—yours and mine."

How long he remained, lost and deranged, was a mystery. He only knew he had survived and now must learn from the costly lesson. He once thought himself invincible but now he knew evil was a real and powerful force in the world. If one should tempt it, either out of curiosity or ignorance, he might well lose his soul and, indeed, his very life.

The priest's parting words from Stonehenge hovered in his memory. "Though the forces for evil be strong, you can influence that which works for good if you fail not the challenges of your destiny."

When he regained consciousness Gisela was gone. He hoped with all his heart she was allowed to return as priestess in the sacred domain near Stonehenge. He was filled with gratitude. The power of their love had summoned her to him in his great peril. Egar emerged, much changed.

Bega helped Itta nurse Egar back to health. With nourishing broths and proximity of caring nurses, his strength grew daily. His soul took longer. Not even their attentions could divert him from his dark brooding.

Chapter Sixteen

One day a messenger arrived. The nobles of Austrasia requested Pepin to call a *conventus generalis* —the annual bringing together of noblemen, leaders, priests and freemen—a tradition buried deep in the past, before they had a hereditary king. In those times, the wandering and warlike Germanic tribes met together each spring to decide which battles to join and who would lead them.

Clothar II had changed the Assembly from a purely military meeting to one where questions of civil and ecclesiastical issues could be aired and discussed. But for the nobles of Austrasia to call a *conventus* in the absence of the king was something that had never before been done.

Pepin was ecstatic. Perhaps the nobles were ready for a new, non-Merovingian king. Soon every family in the realm was preparing for the meeting to be held in Metz.

Bega talked earnestly to Itta, finally winning her approval. That night Itta spoke to Pepin.

"Bega requests permission to be married during the *conventus.*"

"She is but a baby," objected Pepin.

"Though young, barely twelve, she *is* betrothed and a few months more or less will matter little. You must admit, there is precious little social life here now. If we have the wedding while the nobles, priests, and their followers are here, it will seem more festive."

Pepin finally agreed, albeit reluctantly. The wedding would be held prior to the Assembly.

Kyrie eleison, Christe eleison, Kyrie eleison,
Lord have mercy, Christ have mercy, Lord have mercy.

The solemn voices of the monks rose, filling the church with their clear sound as the ancient Greek words began the Mass.

The cathedral at Metz was crowded to overflowing. Not since the court moved had there been such a throng. Itta looked around at the gathering and nodded in contentment. Bega was right. To hold the wedding for the pitifully few people left in Metz, would have been depressing.

It still seemed strange to have the Mass conducted by the new bishop of Metz rather than the familiar Arnulf.

Agnus Dei qui tollis peccata mundi,
Lamb of God who takes away the sins of the world.
... dona nobis pacem.
... give us peace.

As the notes quivered and faded away into the shadows of the cathedral, the worshipers stirred. The bishop declared, *"Ita missa est."*

After the Mass, Bega and Ansegisel went forward and were quietly married, attended by Itta and Pepin, Grimwald and Egar. Following the ceremony, Bega led a willing Ansegisel out to the meadow where a city of open air tents had grown seemingly overnight. A lively scene met their eyes. Banners flapped in the breeze. People of all stations and dress milled about, calling to one another.

On hearing that the bride and groom were among them, everyone wanted to wish the young couple well, offering them flowers as symbols of fertility.

Someone played a few notes on a wooden flute. Another began accompanying the clear melody with a dance rhythm played on a tambourine. A girl began to sway to the music and soon others joined in. Ansegisel pulled Bega into the dance.

Bega in her finest dress, flowers in her flowing dark hair, adored dancing arm in arm with Ansegisel. His cheeks flushed with exertion and love for her shone in his eyes. They stomped, stepped, and twirled to the sound of the music. Villeins, freemen and slaves, men and women, peasants and high born, joined in the celebration.

By the time the bridal pair arrived at the great hall, breathless and disheveled, it was filled with nobles invited to the feast. Bega and Ansegisel stopped in surprise. Since Dagobert's move to Paris, they had become used to a drab room with scarcely enough people to fill a second trestle table at the mid-day meal. Today no one would guess the king and his queen no longer dwelt in Metz. The hall was resplendent once again with banners and wall hangings brought by each of the noblemen attending the *conventus.* Flowers graced the corners of the room as well as the huge tables laden with both hearty and dainty foods.

When they finished eating a call went up for Egar to entertain. Although far removed from the famished and ill young man who had stumbled in from the forest, he was still quite weak. Many gasped to see him so gaunt and pale. Still they wanted a song, if he were able.

"At Dagobert and Gomatrud's wedding you sang of the Merovingians, descendant from a serpent. Will you not sing of Arnulf and Pepin for this wedding of their offspring?"

"Yes, yes! Sing us Pepin's Song," cried the wedding guests.

Egar went to the great harp and, having tuned its strings, swept a chord like dew drops falling on crystal. There was still magic in the instrument—when Egar played it.

"My lords, ladies," Egar said, bowing, "you ask for Pepin's Song. Songs such as that have a time to be born, a time to fly. Pepin's Song is still somewhere in the unseen future. I will sing the song that *has* been born this day."

Egar once again stroked his harp. The silence fairly quivered.

He sang of a young maiden so lovely and so full of life that everyone in the kingdom loved the very ground she trod. He sang of the one young nobleman, so gifted in intelligence and honor, so handsome to gaze upon, so gentle yet strong that he, among all the men of the realm, won her heart.

He sang of the betrothal and the wedding celebrated in cathedral, field and hall. Of their future filled with love and respect one for the other. Of a child of their loins who would one day be born and named Pepin after her father. The son would continue the greatness of the family, so richly endowed, so admired by all.

The harp's heavenly sound hung suspended above the listeners long after the last word was sung. When he finished, Egar's voice was husky with the strain of singing. His brow glistened with sweat. His cheeks were pale. He had spent freely of his feeble strength in this, his song. It was the only wedding treasure he could offer.

Two days later the hall filled once again, though not so full as it had been for the wedding feast. As mayor of the palace, Pepin sat in the chair of authority on the raised dais. Grimwald was there and Chunibert, the new bishop from Cologne. An Austrasian, he would have a vote. Besides owning vast estates of his own, he managed the church's properties as well. His knowledge was accepted with good will.

In addition to the nobles and priests, a few of the more prominent freemen attended. They would have no vote, but it promised to be a lively discussion.

"We need a king," said Alcuin from his place at the table.

"We have a king," responded Boethius strongly.

"But he is in Paris," Gaiseric said.

"We need a king in *Austrasia*," said Alcuin more forcefully.

"Why need we a king here?" argued Willibald. "We have Pepin."

At this Pepin allowed himself a small smile. He was not yet ready to enter the discussion. He wanted to give the men freedom to speak their thoughts and see how the wind blew before offering himself as their king.

"Mayor of the Palace be stronger than Dagobert anyway," came a voice from the group of freemen standing together along the walls.

Everyone turned to see who had spoken, but the voice came out of the crowd and its owner did not push to make himself recognized.

"With the king gone, too many people be moving away," complained another of the freemen.

This met with a general clamor of agreement.

"Time was, people be coming from all around. Now no one comes to market. If none buys, Metz dies."

"Perhaps we need a new king," observed Pepin, quietly. "One who knows and respects Dagobert, but who could lead the Austrasians as he once did when Clothar was on the throne in Paris."

"But who could that person be?"

Eyes looked around the great hall, resting briefly on the figure of Pepin, then skittering away.

"There be none here with royal blood."

Pepin could not believe they would still choose their king solely because he had Merovingian blood in his veins. How could they be so blind as to prefer a man who had never been a decisive force in Austrasia just because he had descended from a 'royal' family?

He clenched his teeth trying to keep his expression impassive. A flush of anger heated his neck and face. His hands instinctively made fists as if to ward off a physical blow.

"We need a promise from Dagobert to divide his time equally between Paris and Metz," continued the nobles, pretending not to notice Pepin's discomfort.

In the end, Pepin, as Mayor of the Palace, was charged to go to Paris to secure Dagobert's acceptance of their proposal. The Austrasians were not interested in a new non-Merovingian king. Not yet.

Chapter Seventeen

Egar and Grimwald joined the half dozen soldiers accompanying Pepin on his journey to Paris.

"When, Egar?" Pepin asked impatiently. "When will the vision be fulfilled? When will I be king?"

"I do not know."

"But it will happen? It was a true vision, not some childish hallucination?" Pepin persisted.

"A true vision, I am sure of that, but…"

"But what?"

Egar hesitated. Pepin wondered what problems lay ahead.

"All I can tell you is I saw the vision. There was a crown, and tremendous power, strength… impossible to explain. Nevertheless, I knew then, as I do now, that vision was of a great king, and he will come to rule the Franks."

Pepin felt a surge of triumph.

Egar continued, "I know not when it will come to pass. Nor what trials will occur before it does. I only know if it *is* you who will be king, you must be ready."

At last the party saw Mont Sainte-Geneviéve in the hazy distance. The buildings of Paris were escaping their island prison and beginning to cluster around the monasteries on the left bank like chicks around a setting hen.

Pepin's heart beat more rapidly. What problems would he meet at the palace? He knew much had changed. Dagobert was no longer a child and he the honored tutor. Was there still respect? Would Dagobert acquiesce to the demands of the Austrasians? With a sigh, Pepin hurried his mount forward, the rest of the men setting their pace to his.

The horses clattered across the bridge onto the île de la Cité.

Pepin, Grimwald and Egar were surprised to find the great hall in disarray. Although coming upon midday, servants were still cleaning what looked to be the results of festivities held the previous night. When they inquired, they were told Dagobert was still in his chamber. They would be welcome to see him there.

They were shocked to find the king still in his rumpled bed just breaking his fast. He had gained weight. His face was puffy, his eyes bloodshot. He had the grace to laugh apologetically, gesturing them to take seats on the bench.

"Welcome to Paris. We had a rather..." the monarch raised an eyebrow, "merry time last night, which lasted well into today. Ah, well. One must grasp pleasure where one can, must one not?"

The Austrasian's were at a loss for words. Where was the energetic, likable young king they had sent to Paris less than twelve short months ago? This man was a complete stranger.

Dagobert seemed not to notice the embarrassed silence. "Well, gentlemen, what brings you to court?"

Grimwald and Egar looked at Pepin. He took a moment before saying, "Sire, you are sorely missed in Austrasia. We bring sincere wishes for your health."

Dagobert smiled. "We thank our loyal and beloved subjects of Austrasia for their kind thoughts."

The courtly words clashed with his disheveled appearance.

"Sire, the nobles of Metz have sent us," continued Pepin in his most diplomatic voice. "You are missed— you, the lovely Queen Gomatrud and young Sigibert. Metz, and indeed all of Austrasia, is not the same without you. We urge you, return to Metz if only for a portion of the year."

"That is out of the question for Gomatrud." The king shrugged. "But I might consider a short visit some time in the future. After all," Dagobert smiled, though his eyes remained aloof, "I should see you do not grasp too much authority in our eastern province. Am I right?"

Dagobert gave no space for a reply. "Now I must be up and dressed. I shall look forward to seeing you for the evening meal."

With that they were ushered out of the chamber. They stood, stunned into disbelief. What had so changed their monarch?

With time on their hands and no offer of food or drink, they made their way to a nearby inn where they ordered ale, bread, sausage and cheese.

"Dagobert looks terrible," said Grimwald.

"And his reference to it being 'out of the question' for Gomatrud to come to Metz," said Egar. "What was the meaning of that?"

"Perhaps she is expecting another child," Grimwald replied.

"But if that were true," said Pepin, "would not Dagobert have boasted of the fact? No, I think there is something else here."

As they ate they were joined by other customers of the inn. They had no need to prod for information. Local gossip was the sole topic of conversation.

The young queen had been supplanted by at least one mistress, perhaps more. With what dignity she could muster she had elected to quit the court and enter a monastery.

"That explains it!" Pepin tried to controll his anger. "What choice had she? Gomatrud could hardly have returned home a failure after the dowry had been delivered and the nuptials celebrated."

"How many tears she must have shed in the privacy of her chamber," Egar commented. "I wonder if any of her ladies-in-waiting have chosen to share her cloistered condition."

Grimwald shrugged. "If any do remain at court, I wager they are only too willing to serve whoever takes the queen's place!"

Egar sighed. "How sad."

Pepin and Grimwald nodded.

"Remember how beloved Gomatrud was in Metz?" asked Grimwald.

Pepin pushed away his trencher, the food only half-eaten. "It is hard to picture her sequestered behind high walls, deprived of love, unable to watch her son become a man."

Dinner that night was an embarrassment to the delegates from Metz. The queen's chair was pointedly empty, but a very well-endowed young lady with long red curls framing a spectacular face coquetted outrageously with the king. She caressed him in the most intimate way and fed him tidbits from their shared trencher. In fact, an abundance of females graced the hall. Hardly a nobleman, guard, scribe or priest lacked a comely young maiden with whom to share a trencher.

The three from Metz sat above the salt but far enough from the king to be unable to converse with him. They murmured quietly among themselves, no one paying them the slightest heed.

"This flaunting of whores is most unseemly." Disgust roiled in Pepin's belly.

"I've never seen anything like it in Metz," agreed Grimwald.

"Nor was there in Paris under Clothar, that I remember," added Egar.

Wine flowed. Voices grew louder, punctuated with girlish giggles and robust male laughter.

Some peasant musicians played a lively tune on pipes, drum and tambourine. The diners clapped and cheered as one of the girls, moving to the music, swayed sinuously.

"I can see why that one is such a favorite with the men," said Grimwald.

"It is clear she intends her performance to be an invitation to the bedchamber," Pepin replied. "I wager few men of Dagobert's court go to solitary pallets after evenings such as this."

"By the gods, others are joining her in the dance! How do they manage to bend their bodies so... so... intriguingly?" Grimwald asked.

"I know not where to look, that does not make me feel I intrude upon their privacy." Egar blushed as he spoke.

"The evening is a veritable Roman bacchanal," Pepin fumed. "I can *not* understand such behavior being accepted at court. By God, how can Dagobert condone it?"

The three pushed aside their bench and wended their way out of the pulsing hall. Pepin looked back and slammed his fist against the door jam. "Not one person there even noticed we have left! Least of all, Dagobert!"

"Nor would they care, if they had," murmured Egar.

Several days later, Pepin finally managed to get Dagobert to agree to go out riding.

"Your majesty," Pepin began, "your loyal subjects feel it is most important that you come to Austrasia. We realize running Neustria and Burgundy adds to your burden and that Paris offers many entertainments, but you are responsible for all your kingdom. Austrasia is not the least of your domain. Might you not spend at least half of the year there?"

The smile vanished from Dagobert's flushed face. "How dare you tell me what to do! I will rule my kingdom, *all of it,* as I see fit. You are no longer my tutor—and I no longer your student.

"Return you to Metz. Tell my nobles, if they wish to see me, they must come to Paris. It is my pleasure to live here, and by the faith, I will do whatever I choose! No one, you least of all, is going to tell me how to conduct my life!"

Pepin was thunderstruck by this unwarranted attack.

"If you are unable to make them accept my wishes in this regard," the king shouted, "I shall replace my mayor of the palace in Metz with someone who can!"

With that Dagobert turned his horse hard and galloped back to the palace. Pepin and the royal guards followed, dumbfounded by his inexplicable outburst.

Chapter Eighteen

A cloud of despondence hung over the nobles and priests assembled in the great hall in Metz. With one look at Pepin's face, they knew Dagobert was not returning to Austrasia. They were angry as well. How dare they be ignored! Their kingdom was as important to the Merovingian empire as any. Did the fault lie with Dagobert or with Pepin? They had men and wealth, and, by God they would not sit idly by and watch their power disappear without a fight!

Pepin wished he could report success from his Paris trip. But seeing the anger so near the surface, he thought perhaps it was just as well he could not. If they could be turned against Dagobert...

"My lords, the king will not consider leaving Paris. And in some ways, that is not the worst of what I have to report."

He went on to tell them in graphic detail how changed the king was since moving to Paris. There were loud murmurs from the assembled men, some of dismay, others of disbelief, as Pepin revealed the debauchery at court and how Gomatrud had been forced into a convent.

"Dagobert is no longer an Austrasian," he declared. "He has become a Neustrian and adopted the worst of Roman ways."

"I doubt it is as bad as Pepin has reported," claimed Grimo. "He would like us to forswear Dagobert in order to gain more power for himself."

Many of the noblemen who supported Pepin, shouted Grimo down in outrage, but a few of them looked at Pepin in speculation. He could read their thoughts. *Was* Pepin the Vain trying to usurp the king's place?

Grimo, smaller than most and perpetually finding slights where none were intended, was known for his hot temper. However, he did have followers. They, like him, fought first and thought last, if ever.

"We all know Dagobert. He is a fine enough king. If any of *us* had asked for his return, he would have honored our request," said Grimo's cousin Adalgisel.

Benches crashed to the floor as several men hastily stood, snarling in readiness for a fight. Pepin, himself, felt a nearly uncontrollable urge to land a fist in Adalgisel's slimy mouth.

Grimwald stood. "Honored council! I was there with my father. Believe me, it is just as he reported. Ask Egar, ask anyone who was there. You would not recognize Dagobert. And Gomatrud, the true queen, is gone. All Paris is talking about her expulsion from the court."

"Of course Grimwald would support his father," came Grimo's reply. "Even Egar is in his hand. They would swear the moon was blue for Pepin, if he asked it."

"Why not summon the guards who were with them and ask how they saw conditions there?" suggested Alcuin.

The combatants stopped in place, blows barely averted. Pepin took a deep breath. He dared not catch Alcuin's eye with his thankful look. Others might interpret it as collusion. Instead he thanked God for all reasonable men.

A page was sent running to the guardhouse to bring back witnesses to verify or repudiate Pepin's report. Meanwhile men righted their benches and returned to their places.

Shortly the page returned, followed by two of the guards hastily buckling on belts and setting caps in place.

"You wanted us, m'lords?" one of them asked as they halted to stand respectfully before Pepin.

"Yes, Euric," said Pepin. "The men assembled here would like to hear from your own lips, how you found conditions at court."

The two guards exchanged worried glances. Tension in the air was measurable. Pepin knew they were loyal and wished he could give them a clue as to what sort of reply he wanted. But, he could not.

When the silence became unbearable, the guards had no recourse but to tell truthfully what they had seen. They confirmed all Pepin had said. They even added a few colorful words heard bandied about the barracks describing Dagobert's court.

Pepin smiled. "Thank you for your report. You may return to your duties."

The guards bowed to Pepin. Then they turned and looked at the assembled noblemen as if measuring which of them would dare to oppose their leader.

Nothing further could be done. Many in the hall stamped off, clearly unhappy with the report.

Pepin spent the summer working throughout the province. Time and again he packed his saddlebags and left on whirlwind inspections of all Austrasia. His party, a tight knot of swiftly moving sweaty men and horses, traveled dusty roads into every corner of the realm. He examined mills, granaries, bridges and the like, to insure they were maintained in perfect repair.

Wherever he went, Pepin settled disputes in the name of the crown.

"The cow was stolen!"

"No, it was found!"

"No, it was a gift."

He ruled on the amount of money or goods that must trade hands to resolve the matter.

One neighbor accused another of a crime—Pepin ordered the trial to determine guilt or innocence. The accused might swear an oath administered in church on the Gospel or a religious relic. If it were trial by ordeal, he might have to plunge his arm into boiling water to retrieve an object. If his arm and hand healed without a scar at the end of several days, he was proven innocent.

The guards complained as they traveled constantly. But Pepin felt if he kept moving fast enough, nothing bad could catch up with him. If he slept in his own bed more than two nights running he suffered anxiety and raced off again to the outermost parts of the province.

Chapter Nineteen

Grain ripened from green to gold in the fields. Days began to shorten. In the darkness before dawn of an early autumn morn men gathered in the bailey outside the royal residence in Metz.

Pepin called out. "Mount up!" and took his place at the head of the group.

He experienced a feeling of exhilaration, which along with the crisp chill of fall, made him feel vitally alive. After all the journeys he had made in the heat and dust of summer, he was about to harvest the fruits of his extraordinary efforts. Seeing the bounty of the land collected would make him feel almost a king already.

With the sun high overhead, they pulled into the first farm. A sorry affair, it boasted a small dark hovel on a strip of barren, unyielding land. The family who lived there were villeins—poor peasants but freemen, not slaves. Three days each week they worked on the king's land near the river. The rest they spent on their own poor strip, struggling to grow enough to keep starvation at bay.

"Good marrow, m'lords," said the old man. "Ye be coming for King Dagobert's share o' me labors."

"Aye." Pepin pitied the man's unenviable position. Ah well, he thought, some were born to rule and some to toil in ignorance and poverty.

"It be stored yonder. No need haul it here. We no be having the use o' it. It do seem the very soil knows it be the king's and grows only that which be fit for a royal table, not for the likes o' we."

Riding farm to farm, they stopped to slake their thirst with ale brewed by a hearty widow. Single-handedly, she rolled casks out to the wagon, her tribute to the king. She tapped a hogshead for Pepin and the men.

"When Dagobert were here," complained the widow to Pepin, "there be customers aplenty. Time was, with the king close-by, there be people stopping by for ale every day. They brung flour, potatoes, sometimes even a side of bacon to exchange for a cask to take home with 'em."

"But—" Pepin tried to interject.

"In them days—" she didn't even pause for breath, "—when we had a king, there be fairs and market days aplenty where I betimes even made a coin or two selling drinks to them what had money. But now there be no one to drink and no one to pay."

She sighed gustily, refilling Pepin's empty mug. "This winter I leave the business for good. Me mate started it and the ale saw all our brood through good times and bad but now, with him gone these five years past, there be no choice for me but to move in with me son and his family."

Will she never run out of words? Pepin wondered, exasperated.

"There be not enough food traded for ale this year to keep a goat alive. Next year no more ale for the king will ye get from me 'cause I won't be making it. I can't give what I ain't got."

Pepin recalled the gaiety that had permeated the countryside when he rode out with Dagobert. Now, they met nothing but grumbling and poverty.

* * *

They entered the estate where they were to spend the night. With guards posted by the supply wagon, Pepin joined the nobleman's family for the evening meal in the hall.

"Why should we give tribute to a king we haven't seen since Clothar died?" asked the master of the hall.

"If the need arises," answered Pepin, "the king will be here to protect us. Besides, he is just as much our king in Paris as ever he was here."

"If Dagobert chooses not to come to Austrasia now, how do we know he will come to our defense if we are attacked?" demanded the nobleman.

"He will defend Austrasia because we are an important part of his realm," reminded Pepin.

"But not important enough to live here. Or even visit!" complained the nobleman. "I tell you this, Pepin, and you can tell the king for me, if he expects full tribute to be paid he must be full king to us."

Pepin tried to defend Dagobert, but the nobleman was expressing what others had already said.

"I see no reason to give our precious crops and our women's finely woven cloth to a king who chooses to live elsewhere!"

Pepin had nothing left to say.

The estate had more warriors armed with throwing axes and swords than did Pepin on this trip. The lord's word carried weight.

Pepin sighed. There seemed no end to the despair. Anger, building like a storm, threatened to turn the entire domain into an armed conflagration.

Once more in Metz, Pepin searched out Egar. "I plan to spend the winter in Paris," Pepin said. "Will you go with me?"

"Of course, if you wish it. But why do you want to go?"

"To be near the king. Perhaps he grows tired of his corrupt ways. Pleasures of the flesh wane with overuse.

If I am there I can judge when I stand the best chance of success. After all I have seen, it is clear I *must* bring him back to Austrasia, whatever my destiny." Pepin sighed and lowered himself heavily to the bench. He sat, elbow on the table, his chin in his hand.

"Do you give up on the prophecy?" asked Egar.

"I… I hope not. But if I were to think as a king, I must desire the best for my kingdom. What is best for Austrasia is Dagobert in residence here. If the future gives me a chance at the throne, I will be ready and only too eager to grasp it."

"I am not sure spending the winter in Paris will be helpful," Egar said.

Pepin sucked in a breath of air and quickly turned toward him. "Is it the Sight? Have you knowledge against it?"

"No." Egar smiled. "I have no such 'knowledge'. Going to Paris seems pointless and perhaps even dangerous. The king did not wish you well. And to absent yourself from Metz, leaving your enemies free to cause trouble—" he shrugged, "—I am not sure it is wise."

"Come spring," Pepin responded, " if nothing has changed, we will return to mend fences here. In the meantime I want to be near the center of power. There might be aught I can do to further Austrasia's cause… or my own."

"What a wonderful idea," enthused Grimwald when Pepin told the family of his plan later that evening. "I will go with you."

"No. Stay you and take care of your mother."

"Bega and Ansegisel are here. They can tend to her needs."

"They have their own affairs. It is your place to protect your mother and to be ready if anything ill-fated should occur."

"Nothing is going to happen in the middle of winter. You do not want me to go because Paris is exciting."

"And tempting," Pepin concluded for him.

"I would not be tempted to do anything you would not approve," Grimwald countered. "After all, you would be right there. You let Egar go. He could get into just as much trouble as I. Even more."

Egar recalled the women who were so prominent at Dagobert's bacchanalia. The memory of the dancer's sensuous movements gave life to his desire for a companion, a matter never far below the surface of his day to day life. But the dancer's grace as well as the other women's smiles and provocative looks were too well rehearsed. Intended only to gain food for a hungry belly, a warm, dry shelter for naught but the night.

He could not truly imagine sharing his pallet with such as they.

Pepin answered Grimwald. "Though possible, chances are he would not. Besides, he is not my son. You are."

Egar had forgotten how crowded and busy Paris was. After the quiet of backwater Metz, the noise and smells of this city assaulted his senses. Even the palace was a beehive of activity as they rode through the bailey. Every building housed craftsmen and servants to the court. People scurried about intent on their errands. The kitchen buildings emitted wonderful odors that momentarily overcame the stench from the open sewage underfoot.

That night at supper in the great hall they saw the same breathtaking red-haired woman they had seen before. She sat quite possessively in the queen's carved throne next to Dagobert.

"Have we a new queen then," commented Pepin to the man sitting next to him at the table. He tried hard to make his voice convivial.

"Ah yes. The lovely Nanthild. In the past year and a half, she has risen like a shooting star from chambermaid, to maiden of the chamber, to queen. She is a charmer. No one can fault the king's eye for a beauty."

Pepin murmured quietly to Egar, "I wonder how it came about that one such as she, managed to become Dagobert's queen? Dagobert's coming to Paris must have greatly changed the life of 'the lovely Nanthild'..."

Chapter Twenty

Nanthild could have told Pepin, had he asked. She began planning as soon as she heard word of King Clothar's death and the announcement that Dagobert and Gomatrud were moving their court to Paris.

She knew immediately this was her chance to scheme her way into service as chamber maid in the palace. Ladies-in-waiting to the queen were chosen from the nobility, usually life-long friends of the royal family. Chamber maids could come from a lower class if they were daughters of men who had demonstrated unusual fealty or valor. Although her father was a drunk and her mother a drudge, Nanthild realized this change in the royal households offered her a rare opportunity.

Them from Paris will fancy I come with Dagobert and Gomatrud from Metz, she thought to herself. And the Metz servants will guess I already be in service to the court here in Paris!

Nanthild was aware of her exotic appearance— long red hair, pale skin and almond-shaped green eyes. In a society of sturdy brunettes, she knew she had great allure.

When she saw King Dagobert's procession from the top of the wall she knew she must move quickly.

She timed her appearance at the palace when the horses and carts arrived from Metz. She easily entered the building as one of the flurry of people assembled. Making herself helpful unpacking chests and baskets brought in from the bailey, she soon learned the locations of the queen's chambers, the king's domain, and the nursery.

Nanthild noticed one man looking at her intently. He must be a nobleman, she thought, dressed so fine and doing no work. She gave him her most demure but seductive smile. He beckoned her over to him.

"What is your name, child?" he asked.

"Nanthild, m'lord."

"Ah, Nanthild. Very lovely." His words might have referred to her name. His eyes made it clear he was speaking of her body. "Tell me, Nanthild, do you know who I am?"

"No, m'lord," answered Nanthild honestly. "But me thinks ye be someone very fine, dressed as ye are."

"Were you one of Clothar's servants?" he asked.

Nanthild inhaled sharply. This is the test, she realized. If I say I was in Clothar's service and he is one of Clothar's men, he will know I am lying. But he could just as well have come with Dagobert and know I do not belong with them either. She looked into the light blue eyes of the nobleman with the long blond hair and suddenly realized with whom she was speaking. Only the king was allowed long hair.

Her eyes grew large in fright. "Oh, your majesty!" She began to tremble. "I be not knowing I speak to our new king. Welcome to Paris, sire," she added. For all her confusion, her smile gathered courage as it reached her eyes.

"Thank you, Nanthild of Paris." Dagobert's voice was somber but not unfriendly. "I shall not ask what your position at court has been. As of now you may consider yourself a chambermaid to the queen. Does that please you?"

"Oh, yes, sire. And... thank you sire." She curtsied, hoping her trembling legs would not embarrass her further by dumping her to the floor until after he had left.

Just then another nobleman entered the chamber. He moved so smoothly, he seemed to float rather than walk.

"Sire, may I personally welcome you back to Paris." The man bowed. "Gelasius, at your service."

Nanthild noticed while he was not so tall as the king, the arrogance with which he carried himself, made him even more commanding.

"My condolences on the death of Clothar."

He looks not the least bit sad, Nanthild thought. He *was* handsome. Slender body. Brown beard neatly trimmed. Dark hair with just a touch of grey at the temples. Olive-complected face dominated by a large Roman nose.

"I served on his inner council. It having been some years since you lived in Paris, let me guide you through the inevitable pitfalls of reigning among some of our..." Gelasius shrugged expressively, "more contentious subjects."

Everything about him was immaculate, from his shining hair, the wine-red, sleeveless mantle over his white linen shirt, to his soft leather boots. I bet it be clean even under his fingernails, Nanthild thought with disgust.

"Let me show you..."

Gelasius took Dagobert's arm possessively and began leading him to the gallery overlooking the main hall. He turned and noticed Nanthild for the first time. The cold look in his hazel eyes quite took her breath away. She remained frozen in place.

With an expression that clearly told her to return to the dark place from which she had crawled, he continued out the chamber with the king.

The quiet words he spoke were indistinguishable, but she felt sure one of them was "whore". The king's light laughter did little to reassure her.

Nanthild was quite taken by the aloof regal queen. She began mimicking her dainty manners until her family and friends teased her on her rare visits home, calling her "your royal highness" and "your majesty". The teasing bothered Nanthild not one whit. She soon felt more at home in the palace than in the wattle and daub hovel where she had been born. She visited her family less and less often.

Nanthild felt sorry for the queen. The Austrasians seemed a rough and robust lot, speaking a Teutonic dialect among themselves. The Parisians of Neustria had always been more strongly influenced by their Roman heritage, speaking Latin and favoring an indulgent, smoothly civilized lifestyle. Gomatrud might have been at home in Metz, but not in Neustrian Paris. One by one the servants who came with her were replaced by Parisians. Nanthild's job was secure. No one seemed to remember she had not been there all along.

Dagobert, having spent his childhood here, got along splendidly with the seigneurs who took it upon themselves to advise him. His love of women, gambling, fancy foods and wine were, in fact, very Neustrian.

As the months wore on, royal Gomatrud grew ever stiffer and more unyielding. Her once sunny disposition was replaced with a look of strained intolerance. Uncomfortable speaking Latin, she spoke to no one. Consequently, no one spoke to her.

Late one evening a message from the king was whispered into Nanthild's ear. He wished to see her. Now. Quietly. Hurriedly she got out of bed. Slipping her feet into felt slippers and pulling a robe over the chemise in which she slept, she silently followed the messenger.

Before entering service in the palace Nanthild had supplemented her meagre serving wench's earnings by accommodating the men who patronized the tavern where she worked. She knew well what a summons in the middle of the night meant. Nervously she reminded herself that king or not, Dagobert, was still a man.

She found him pacing up and down his large room, trailing behind him a silk mantle that had slipped off his shoulders. His hunting dogs lay watching him as he strode back and forth, sipping wine from a goblet. Nanthild took in the scene with one swift glance.

"Sire," she said quietly, eyes demurely downcast, "you wished to see me?" Nanthild made sure her robe exposed only a small glimpse of her firmly rounded breast.

"Ah, yes. Nanthild, is it?"

"Yes, sire." There was a pause as the king gazed at her, his eyes evaluating her disposition.

"Stand there," he pointed to the middle of the room, "and let me look at you. Turn, slowly."

Nanthild looked him in the eye before showing him her profile and then her back.

"Ah, yes, beautiful."

Not too boldly, she told herself. He will want you willing but not too eager.

"Take off your robe and camise."

She shrugged her shoulders out of the robe, leaving it where it fell in a heap on the floor. She stood, allowing the monarch to examine her. Dagobert's eyes swiftly traveled to the hem of her linen camise—to where the legs of her short underdrawers would have shown, had she been wearing any.

She could not suppress the small smile that crept into her eyes as she noticed his reaction to this. She untied the bow of her camise and pulled it off.

"Very good," the king said. "Now, your slippers."

Slowly she drew off one, and then the other. Nanthild stood, completely naked.

Dagobert sighed in pleasure. No reluctance or shame diminished the impact of Nanthild's nude body. Her creamy skin glowed with the translucence of pearl. Firm full breasts rose above a slender waist. Truly there was not a marble statue in all of Rome to do justice to the one that stood, warm and breathing, before him.

"Yes, I would say you will do very nicely. Now, do you know how to take away a man's... restlessness of spirit?"

"Oh, yes, sire. Sit here." She indicated a comfortable seat.

Dagobert inhaled deeply as Nanthild began to knead the tension out of his neck and shoulders. That first touch of skin to skin elicited a sharp, pleasant tingle. He had not misjudged her. She knew what was needed.

She kissed his eyelids, then his lips, while at the same time peeling off his silken mantle and undertunic.

Dagobert felt the anxiety leave his body. The excitement of his hardening male organ brought with it a sense of purpose and passion that had been missing for many months. Bedding the disapproving Gomatrud had been so unappealing, it had, on the last two occasions, left him impotent. This alarmed Dagobert who prided himself as much for his ability between the sheets as on the battlefield.

With restored arrogance Dagobert quickly stood and faced Nanthild. He let his hands caress her breasts and then slowly work down her body to her slim waist. With both hands, one covering each of her buttocks, he held their feminine roundness, pulling her closer to him until their bodies met—lips, breasts, organ to triangle of hair. Feeling his hardness,

Nanthild began to glow with a radiance that raised Dagobert's excitement to new levels.

He pulled her into bed and thrust into her. No shy, resisting, virgin maid, she welcomed his strokes, giving as well as she got, matching her rhythmic movements to his. He burst, pouring his pungent fluid into her.

They lay for several minutes, panting and sweaty, until Dagobert turned and ran his fingers through her long red hair. He gazed, blue eyes into green. Acceptance and excitement there matched his own. Slowly this time, he caressed her breasts, her body, her beautiful seductive opening and made long, leisurely love.

Chapter Twenty-one

All Paris was talking! Dagobert found beautiful Nanthild a more desirable bed partner than his queen!

Nanthild's family and friends no longer teased her for reaching above her station. She received a sizeable treasure in gifts and trinkets from other girls wanting to be introduced at court. Nanthild brought some of the prettier ones to entertain the men who sat at the trestle tables. But no one was allowed to jeopardize her place in the king's bed! One unlucky girl who tried had her face so permanently scarred by Nanthild's long nails, she lost forever any opportunity she might have had of being a maiden of the chamber.

Word raced through the court. Dagobert had ordered Gomatrud sent to a convent in the countryside. Perhaps he was tired of the charade their marriage had become. Or he wished to rid himself of the disapproval in her eyes, reminding him how different he was now from the loving king he had been when they lived in Metz. Whatever the reason, Gomatrud was forced to give up forever her claim to the throne, her husband and her son.

* * *

Disaster struck Nanthild the following April. For two months she refused to believe it until she could no longer deny the fact. In her womb she carried the king's seed... his bastard.

Her only value to the king was in his bed. How seductive would she appear when her body, sagging and bloated, became heavy with the baby? What would become of them? She and the babe would be thrown out into the streets she had fought so long to escape.

No one in all Paris would be ignorant as to the child's sire. She and it would be cast out like garbage. No one would dare claim or care for them.

Nanthild knew women skilled in the use of herbs. They had potions which would, if she were brave enough to take them, kill the seed growing in her womb. The church adamantly forbade the taking of any such *maleficium*. She would be damned and required to do penance—at least seven years of prayer and fasting—before she could be absolved of such a sin.

She was not as fearful of the church as she was of the king's possible reaction should he find out. If she killed his child, he could take her own life in retribution.

What should she do? If only there were someone she could talk to. Out of the question.

Finally, she decided to tell the king and prepare to leave the palace. Leave Paris. Go so far no one would have heard her name or of their alliance. Start a new life. She had learned pretty manners while in service at the court. Perhaps if she went far enough, she could find employment in some large estate where they had never heard of Nanthild, the king's whore, and her bastard child.

She thought of a thousand reasons to delay telling Dagobert her secret. But soon the life growing within her would begin to show and who could tell, there might be some who were already aware that for two months she had not had her monthly flow. Gelasius was only one of several who were jealous of her privileged place in the king's favor. He would not hesitate to whisper in

Dagobert's ear, delighted to see her banned in disgrace —his own relationship with the king strengthened thereby. One way or another, Dagobert would learn her secret. *She* must be the one to tell him. Tonight.

She washed her body in water scented with floating rose petals. She brushed her hair until it was a shining halo of auburn waves around her face. With trembling fingers she selected a sleeveless gown of soft gold that brought out the highlights in her hair. Then before she lost all courage, she forced reluctant legs to carry her to the king's chamber. His look of pleasure stabbed her like a knife. How could she risk losing the king's patronage? What choice had she?

"Sire, I have something to tell you. When I have finished, I wish to ask your blessing."

Without a word Dagobert drew close behind her. Putting his arms around Nanthild, his hands thoughtlessly became a girdle around the womb that held his child.

"What is it, my beautiful Nanthild? Why so serious? What is it that frets my jewel, my emerald set in burnished gold?"

Nanthild's heart skipped a beat.

"Sire, I have given myself gladly to your pleasure," she began. "Indeed you are my only, my greatest joy."

The king looked perplexed. "Of course."

"But... I am with child! Your child." Nanthild was overwhelmed by a suffocating sadness.

The king turned her around to face him. Her eyes were downcast so she missed seeing his look of incredulous joy. Gently he put a jeweled finger under her chin and lifted her face to his. He kissed her once sweetly before loosing all control. He grabbed her in a strong embrace and nearly smothered her with a kiss of passion.

Tearing himself away he asked anxiously, "You are feeling well?"

"Yes, sire. Very well indeed. But troubled."

"Why troubled? You are blessed above all women to carry the royal Merovingian seed. You should be shouting your joy from the palisade."

"I am honored," Nanthild agreed with her whole heart, "but it is a bastard seed, nonetheless."

"That is of small concern. My child shall be recognized as a legitimate heir to the throne. It has been done before. No one would dare question he has Merovingian blood in his veins."

"I shall keep to my alcove until the child is born and then ask your blessing to leave the court," said Nanthild both relieved and saddened.

"Leave? Why leave? Why keep to your room?"

"You will not wish to see me, heavy and awkward with child. You will desire someone new and beautiful for your bed."

"You will be heavy, though never I think awkward, with *my* child and I desire no one else for my bed. Rather than be confined to an alcove, you should have chambers worthy of a queen as you will bear a king's son." His face brightened. "You shall have the queen's chambers *and* the queen's throne!"

On the coldest day of the year, whispered word raced through the palace. Queen Nanthild had taken to her bed. The birth could not be far off.

The sky was leaden and low, almost touching the rooftops. Shutters banged and leather curtains at windows and doorways flapped stiffly as cold air pushed under and around them, creeping along the floors of the palace.

One of a group awaiting word from the bedchamber laughed. "I do not envy the queen having to 'bare all'— to bear a babe in this weather."

"Nor do I envy the babe to be greeted by such cold hands as the midwife must have," agreed another.

Finally, news. Dagobert had a son. A prince born alive and robust, screamed lustily. The queen was reportedly tired but well, the king entirely pleased. He now had two heirs to the throne. The Merovingian line, descended from a serpent, was secure.

Bonfires set on the tops of hills blazed with the news, spreading it to every corner of the kingdom. Special masses of thanksgiving were conducted as candles of praise burned into the night.

In the palace, the midwife carefully checked the afterbirth for any irregularities and finding none, put the blood-red mass reverently into a special receptacle kept for that purpose. No one asked what she planned to do with it, which was just as well. They would have been shocked to learn it was to be burned along with charms and incantations, to guarantee the blessing of the old gods on this descendent of Clovis, first of the Merovingians to embrace Christianity.

The baby was baptized Clovis II at a celebration mass in the church of Saint Denis. Egar and Pepin stood amid the crush of nobles straining to catch a glimpse of the ceremony.

At the front of the church the baby began to cry and Egar stood on tiptoe trying to see what was happening. He thought nothing of being at the back of the crowd of visitors but he realized with a start Pepin should have been ushered up to the dais where King Dagobert and the Bishop of Paris stood.

Egar looked at Pepin and noticed him wince slightly.

"What is it?" Egar asked.

"Staying here, waiting Dagobert's pleasure—I feel ill-used. The clouds of incense and flickering candles cause my head to ache."

"Perhaps now the baby has been baptized, Dagobert will see you," Egar ventured.

"I can only hope so. Life in Paris grows more intolerable with each passing day. With two heirs to the throne, I cannot see how someone such as I could ever wrest the crown from the Merovingians."

Pepin looked around, quickly. Their conversation had been a whispered one. All attention was to the front—on the squaling babe.

"Be that as it may, I must somehow persuade Dagobert to return with us to Austrasia. I must!"

Chapter Twenty-Two

Day after day Pepin sought an audience with Dagobert. The king was "not well," though he recovered sufficiently to eat and drink late into the night, laughing and trading ribald comments with the men and women nearer the high end of the table. He could keep neither his eyes nor his hands off Nanthild. She welcomed his attentions with provocative looks and gestures that could be easily read well below the salt.

If not unwell, he was "too busy," though he had ample time to ride out with his cronies and followers—after sleeping the morning away.

Pepin, with extraordinary effort, kept his tongue under control until he and Egar could ride out of Paris. They cantered together over the bridge leading across the Seine.

Winter still held the land in its grip. Bare branches formed a chiaroscuro design in the gray mist.

Pepin mimicked bitterly, "'*You will always be welcome at our court... You of Austrasia will always have our ear.*' Did Dagobert not say that before he left?"

Egar agreed. "To be truthful, I am amazed you have not lost your temper. You have done well to avoid making a difficult situation even worse. What was his excuse today?"

"He was unable to entertain me today because bishops have traveled a great distance to have an audience with his most royal person. Of course, they came less far than we, but that is beside the point."

"We have been here so long," commented Egar, "he probably thinks we live here and have, therefore, not traveled at all."

"Whatever he thinks, I *must* get his agreement to come back to Metz. But, by Jove, it had better be soon. I cannot tell you how glad I will be to leave this corrupt and stifling place and return home to Austrasia."

"It was *your* idea to winter here," reminded Egar.

"True, but Paris seems much changed since I served as Dagobert's tutor. I cannot bear the thought of having to remain cooped up in the palace much longer. If you were not with me, I think I should surely loose my mind."

The king's messenger finally summoned his Mayor of the Palace.

"At last!" Pepin beamed over his shoulder, giving Egar a gesture of victory as he left the chamber they shared.

Dagobert's corpulent body filled his large carved chair.

"Greetings, sire, and congratulations on the new prince," Pepin opened.

Dagobert acknowledged Pepin's presence with a slight nod. His face was impassive. "I trust you are enjoying our hospitality."

"Very much, sire. And I hope you will allow us to reciprocate when you come to Metz. Though, of course, you will still be host as it is your palace there as well."

Pepin congratulated himself on getting the request in before Dagobert could divert the conversation. His attention returned to words that stunned him.

"...and so, I am relieving you of your office and appointing a Neustrian as mayor of the palace."

For a moment Pepin felt his heart stop. Could not breathe. Was suddenly cold—though sweat broke out around his tingling hair line.

"But, sire! I do not understand. I have faithfully discharged my duties in Austrasia for many years. Since your departure I have been particularly diligent to do all that was expected of me, and more."

"Just so," countered the king. "It is our understanding you have been 'particularly diligent' as you put it, in order to take power and the throne *from me.*

Pepin looked at the king in dazed confusion.

"I have eyes and ears in the great hall in Metz where you suggested they should have a new king, *'One who knows and respects Dagobert, but who could lead the Austrasians as he once did, when Clothar was on the throne in Paris.'* Were those not your very words? Do you deny them?"

"No... yes... but..." Pepin stuttered, trapped.

"And who but yourself were you promoting to the throne? Why else are you are called 'Pepin the Vain'? You see, I know even that. There is nothing about you I do not know." Dagobert sat back a look of satisfaction on his fleshy face.

Pepin's stomach churned. He misunderstands. No! He understands all too well!

Dagobert's voice cut like a hunting knife. "Though how you expected to gain the throne with absolutely no royal blood running in your veins, especially when I have sired ample heirs, astounds me. I no longer trust you to be mayor of the palace. As of now you are relieved of office."

"You cannot..." Pepin started, then stopped. Dagobert was king. He could do anything he pleased.

"However, I am prepared to be lenient," said the king. "Did I not spare Gomatrud's life and allow her to live safely in a nunnery? I still carry fond memories of you from my youth. And..." Dagobert paused. His chin rested on his hand, eyes staring into the distance beyond Pepin. "You may yet be of some service to me. In the meantime, you will remain in the palace. Here in Paris. At my pleasure."

Pepin was dumb struck. Remain here? A virtual prisoner! How long? Months? Years?

Pepin turned on legs that had become wooden. He stared around the empty hall, a guard standing discretely at the distant door.

"If you have any thought of leaving, I would dissuade you. I have forceful means of persuasion at my disposal. Methods my ancestors found quite successful. And of course, I could still change my mind and see you put to death—painfully."

The walk across the hall, up the stairs and down the gallery to their alcove was the longest of Pepin's life. He feared at any moment his shaking knees would give way. Prayed he would meet no one. Could not think how he would look them in the eye—speak to them—if he did.

When at last he pushed aside the leather curtain in the doorway, Egar cried out in alarm, "Pepin, what is it? You are as white as frost."

Pepin could not speak.

"Sit down, man. Drink some of this." Egar thrust a wine skin into Pepin's hand. "Tell me what Dagobert said."

Haltingly at first, Pepin began...

"You are skilled at coming and going without being noticed," Pepin said, concluding his narrative. "How do you do it? I must find a way to get to my family before anyone in Metz learns I am out of favor. They must leave immediately for our estates in Landen and safety."

"I know passageways that are least traveled and clothing that melts into shadows. But there is more to it than that. Even if we cover your hair, your eyes give you away. Your walk is too full of energy. You were born to lead men in battle, not skulk in shadows. It would never work."

Pepin walked to the wind opening and looked out upon the bailey below. "I must go! The new mayor, especially as he is a Neustrian, will jump at the chance to eliminate anyone who might remind people of me. Some among the nobles of Austrasia will be happy to hear I have been stripped of power. They, too, will want my family removed from possible positions of influence."

"What could they do?"

"Put Itta and Bega into a convent which owes its existence to their patronage," Pepin replied. "They would simply disappear from sight. They could be forced to spend the rest of their lives behind cloistered walls, or worse."

"Or worse!" protested Egar. "What could be worse than that?"

"They could kill Grimwald. Of course the good citizens of Metz might want to keep my family alive— cut off their noses, force them to live as objects of ridicule—proof of my own impotence."

"How cruel!" Egar pictured the lovely Bega with a gaping hole where her nose had been.

"I cannot take the chance." Pepin paced the confines of their small room pounding a clenched fist into his flattened palm. "The family *must* get to our estates in Landen. I must find some way out of the palace tonight, before the king's message reaches Metz."

"Would you go also to Landen?"

"No. That would only keep them in danger. They are safer if I stay... where? Metz? Here? I must confess I have not thought that far."

Egar placed a comforting hand on Pepin's shoulder.

Pepin saw his own concern mirrored in his friend's eyes. "Dagobert has pledged me safety as long as I remain here. He is no longer the eager young pupil but on the other hand, as long as I am under his watch, he is also under mine. Perhaps this is the best place for me. Somehow I must warn my family to flee and then return undetected here to Paris, as hostage to their safety. You *must* help me. School me in magic—or even sorcery."

"Magic would not help you, even if you had the time to perfect the skill. And sorcery is a gift. A double-edged sword of the gods. I think not even I am such—"

"By the bull!" Pepin thrust Egar's hand away. "There must be a way. Show me it." His rage mounting, he felt ready to crash his way out of the palace by force, if necessary.

"I was about to say there is a way and—"

"Good! Show me and be quick. I have precious little time."

"You must stay—

"No! I must go, immediately—" Pepin interrupted.

"*I* shall go," Egar finished.

Pepin froze in place. He looked incredulously at Egar. "You would place yourself at risk for me?"

"Of course. Though it is as much for them as you."

Pepin returned to his bench with a sigh. "You may be right." Did Egar realize the chance he took?

"It is imperative no one realize you have gone. Could you leave, get to Metz in the middle of winter in time to warn my family with no one the wiser?"

"I will figure a way. Give me time to ponder." Neither man moved. The wooden building creaked. The torch sputtered. "As long as I leave my traveling cloak on its accustomed peg, I will seem to be here also."

"Jupiter's balls! It is freezing out there! You will never make it to Metz without a cloak."

"I will make it," Egar replied. "I must."

"But how?"

"Leave that to me."

Pepin jerked to his feet, knocking the bench over. "Grimo and his cousin Adalgisel have led the king to distrust me. I swear by Mithras, god of all soldiers, they will suffer! No matter the consequences, on my oath I will see them burn in hell!"

He turned to Egar. "Now go. Tell my family I... tell them only they must take extraordinary caution and obey your every command."

Chapter Twenty-Three

Egar powdered a small dried root and sprinkled it over one serving of the royal guards' food. Then, waiting in the shadows of the barracks, he had only to watch to see which one became too ill to ride out on the morrow's drill.

He felt some pity for the randomly chosen man who would suffer excruciating cramps, loose bowels and vomit, but no long-term effects from the potion. Egar felt sure the gods would one day even the score.

In the darkest hour of the night when all but the afflicted man were asleep, Egar chose an extra uniform from the suffering man's clothes chest. The soldier was too ill to notice the shadowy figure and would have thought it the devil come to gloat over his suffering if he had.

Egar saddled a horse and silently led it out the stable, and across the bailey to a long unused back gate. The hinges had been rubbed with tallow so they made not a sound as the gate was slowly opened. Egar found it no great feat to lock the gate again, once he and the horse were on the other side.

Beyond the palace walls Egar had no need for stealth. Disguised in uniform and on a guard's mount, he must ride as if on the king's own business.

The horse's hooves clattered loudly on the cobblestone streets of Paris. Buildings were closed and shuttered against the freezing air. No light showed through the cracks. No cry or laughter sounded. The city slept.

Egar wrapped his scarf around his neck and lowered his face against the bitter cold. This and his wool cap pulled down around his ears made it unlikely anyone would recognize him.

"King's business! Open the gate!" he shouted to the guard as he barely slowed at the wall.

The guard jumped up from the flickering fire and opened the small door within the huge city gate. It was barely wide enough for one mounted rider to pass through. Within moments Egar's horse pounded hollowly across the bridge. Ahead he saw naught but darkness, unlit by even so much as a sliver of moon or pinprick of stars.

Egar kept to the main roads. As one mount tired, he stopped at farms and estates to trade it for a fresh one, accepting biscuits, cheese, flasks of wine, as was due a soldier of the king. Nowhere he stopped was there any hint of trouble or change. The king's messengers had not yet come with news of the new appointment for the palace in Metz.

Some days later, Egar arrived in Metz, mud spattered and exhausted, scarcely having slept the entire way. He ached from the constant jarring of each new mount.

Once in Metz he was in known territory and found no difficulty getting into the palace enclosure undetected. There, a groom loyal to Pepin's family, pleased, but apparently not surprised by anything Egar might do, took the sweating animal into the stable.

"Not one word of my arrival or I swear you will suffer a magic spell to which I have already forgotten the antidote," Egar threatened.

The servant made a sign against the evil eye and nodded mutely.

Egar made his way to Pepin's family living quarters. He silenced the page with a motion. On entering he found Itta, Grimwald, Bega and Ansegisel sitting at the table. They gasped as they saw him standing just inside the shadows of the doorway.

In a whisper Egar quickly told the family all that had befallen Pepin. He assured them of Pepin's love and plan for their safety—flight being the only reasonable solution.

"We will pack and be ready to leave at first light," Grimwald declared.

"No, you must be ready before daylight."

"How long have we, then?" asked Itta.

"Within the hour. Dress warmly. Take only what you can wear and carry in saddlebags. News of the change in mayors must be traveling this way. I know not how soon it will arrive. You should be at least a full day's journey away before anyone suspects you are gone."

Without panic or further argument they scurried for their chambers. They put on as many layers of clothing as they could and packed jewels, candlesticks and a few precious scrolls into saddlebags.

In the meantime Egar instructed the page to summon the guard Gelimer and quietly bring him to the living quarters.

"M'lord, Egar," said Gelimer. "Ye be sending for me?"

"How well do you love Pepin and his family?" Egar watched the man's eyes and expression carefully.

"Like they was me own. Only, of course, more important."

"Pepin himself has sent me to insure the safety of Lady Itta and the others. Changes are in the air that bode ill for them, I fear," explained Egar. "Will you ride with them to Landen and safety with no word to anyone?"

"And be glad of it. Not only in service to Pepin, but to return to Landen meself to see me wife and young 'uns living there on Pepin's estates."

Egar breathed a sigh of relief. He had remembered the man correctly and chosen wisely.

"Saddle five horses without gaining anyone's attention. Take Pepin's family to a little-used back gate to which the page will lead you. Once out of the castle compound, can you get the whole party outside the walls of Metz without alerting the guards on the city gates?"

"Yes, m'lord," Gelimer replied. "Me cousin be on duty on the east one. He be knowing when to keep his mouth shut."

"Excellent! Hurry. Be ready to ride as soon as the family finishes packing." Turning to the page Egar asked, "Know you the gate I mean?"

"Yes m'lord," the lad replied with confidence.

"As soon as the family is safely out, lock it behind them. Then go to the main gate. I hope no one from Paris will arrive for at least a day or two but we must be prepared for the worst. Let me know immediately if anyone comes. You may not get much sleep this night."

"That is of no importance, sir. If not for Pepin's influence, I would not be here at all."

Well within the allotted time, the page led Itta, Grimwald, Bega and Ansegisel down the servant's stairs to the waiting Gelimer and their horses.

Egar was exhausted from the long ride with too little sleep, yet must stay awake a few hours longer making plans to mask the family's departure. Then and only then could he risk getting some badly needed rest.

In what seemed no more than a few moments, the page scurried in and whispered in a breathless voice, "The family is safely off, but oh, my lord, they are here already from Paris! Two of the king's messengers have ridden in and gone directly to the home of Grimo. What will we do?"

"Curl up on the pallet near the door where you would normally sleep and stall anyone who comes as long as you can," directed Egar. "It might take you some minutes to fully come awake. Am I not right?"

"Yes, sir! It can take a long time when I am deep asleep." The page grinned.

"Once the men are admitted, keep your face averted and enter not the room yourself," admonished Egar. "Leave, if you can, and lose yourself among the sleeping pages that are not on duty tonight. Your best defense is to keep from being recognized by any of Grimo's men. If you cannot leave, keep your wits about you and look to your own welfare. I cannot promise to protect you."

"I can take care of myself," assured the page.

Egar's mind was in a whirl. How did the messengers get here so fast? Grimo's battle-hardened men will capture the family before they can escape Metz! Once apprehended, not only their lives, but Pepin's and mine as well are forfeit.

How long can I stall the men? They must not follow the family this night! Even free of Metz, Itta and Bega will not be able to ride as fast as the guards who pursue them. With a sickening feeling he pictured them, believing themselves free of danger, overtaken and captured on the dark forest road.

There was a commotion at the door and a gruff voice cried, "King's messengers with news. Let us enter!"

He heard the barely discernable murmur of the page's voice and the snarl of the men demanding he allow them entrance and be fast about it. Egar's mind searched frantically for some way out of the dilemma. What could he do? He must think of something.

An idea flashed in his mind. Involving deep magic, it might work. But could he martial his forces, tired as he was? And the aftermath? He would pay for the power, as he always did, with nausea, headache and weakness. How could he save himself and make the perilous journey back to Paris if he spent all of his reserves on the illusion he had in mind?

The alternative was worse. At least this way Itta and the rest stood a chance of surviving. He would have to gamble his own life. Egar stilled his rushing thoughts to send a prayer to his gods for strength and skill.

With a wave of his hand, Egar dimmed the torches to a faint glow. Standing in the middle of the room he concentrated his thoughts on the task ahead.

Egar called forth magical fire that exploded in showers of sparks which hung in the air around its source. As Grimo and the soldiers entered, Egar created tongues of blue flame that shot outwards from his feet, keeping the men at a distance. To *their* bedazzled eyes he wore his magic cloak of black and gold. They did not notice his rumpled, mud-spattered soldier's uniform.

The men stopped short, their eyes nearly as wide as their mouths. They made hand signs against the evil eye no Christian would admit to knowing.

"But, but, Egar," sputtered Grimo, "I thought you in Paris with the king."

Using his deepest, most resonant voice, Egar said slowly, "My body *is* in Paris. You see naught but the spirit which leaves the body to wander the earth in protection of those in need."

"I... is... Pepin with you?" asked one of Grimo's men.

"Naturally. With me in Paris. Where else would he be?"

"That is true, my lord," said one of the royal messengers. "Both Pepin and Egar are in the palace of the king. I have seen them there with my own eyes."

"Wh... what do you here?" asked Grimo.

"I know the message these soldiers of the king have brought. It needs not sorcery to understand why the message went directly to you."

"You already know the news? These men have ridden like prophets from hell to bring it to Metz! How could you already know?" asked Grimo skeptically.

"Ask not how a magician knows what he does," responded Egar gravely. "Those whom you seek are asleep. See for yourselves. You wish to keep them under your control until a council can decide their fate. Leave them for the night. The king's news—and yours—can wait until daylight."

With that Egar withdrew to one side of the room, allowing the men to pass and peer fearfully into each chamber. There the half light revealed, in every bed, a mound under the covers seeming to sleep peacefully.

"We have seen," muttered Grimo. "But I post the king's soldiers and my own guards. Where will you be?"

"Though you will not see it, my spirit will be here, for their protection. My body remains in Paris where it may be seen at any time."

As they retreated, Egar felt his knees buckle. His skin prickled wet and cold with sweat. With this release of concentration the flames died and he stood in the middle of the room, an exhausted man in a borrowed, mud-spattered uniform. Fortunately, the soldiers never looked back.

No one paid any attention to a rumpled figure in the uniform of a king's soldier who hurried out of the palace to the necessary place. There Egar was overcome by nausea. The purging of his body came suddenly in waves, vomit and flux of the bowels, so he was hard put which end to minister to first. Too weak to stand or walk, he was nearly crushed by the ache in his head.

"Deep magic takes great power," his old master had told him when he suffered the aftermath of his first attempt at the god-given art, "leaving exhaustion in its wake."

At last the worst was over and Egar stumbled to his own alcove. He must leave Metz before daylight. The family would not have the full day's lead over the guards he wished but he had given them the night.

He dared not light a fire. By sense of touch alone in the dark he found the potion he sought. Holding the flask in his cold and shaking hands, Egar took a deep breath and concentrated his thoughts. Just as he was about to give up the effort, he felt the liquid become warm with heat that grew without flame.

Pulling on his wool cap and scarf, he returned to the fire the guards had started outside the door.

"They sent me with some hot wine to warm you," he said in a neutral voice. "You have ridden a long way."

"Far enough for me," grumbled one of the guards in the uniform of the palace in Paris.

"Bless you!" Another reached for the offered cup.

"Mithras knows, we can use something warm," added a third guard, in the uniform of Metz.

"This fire is all but useless," the first added.

Egar gave them each a draught of his potion guaranteed to cause deep, dreamless sleep.

Once all snored loudly, Egar retrieved his horse from the stable and hoisted his weak and trembling body onto its back. He was barely able to keep from falling. Only the pounding of his heart gave him the strength to cling to its mane as he rode out the palace enclosure through the same hidden gate the family had used. He locked it securely with his last ounce of strength and magic after he was safely on the other side. He did not want to be around when Grimo found the soldiers asleep and Pepin's family safely away.

Egar swayed dangerously and the feeling of nausea grew in his bowels once again as the horse headed for the east gate. Please, gods, give me strength and luck to get outside the walls of Metz, he prayed.

Mist swirled, nearly obscuring the town wall and its eastern gate. Egar shook with cold and exhaustion.

"Are you the cousin of Gelimer?" Egar's voice was a hoarse whisper.

"Aye, that I be," replied the guard.

"I am... a friend. Open the gate, if you would. I must be gone."

"Of course, m'lord," replied the guard. "But be ye sure ye can ride this night? Ye look unwell to me. I could see ye sheltered until morn. No one need know."

"I thank you for your kind thoughts, but I must... " Egar swallowed, "I must not be in Metz when daylight comes."

"Very well, m'lord. May the gods watch over ye," cried the guard as he opened the small night doorway in the gate.

Not wanting anyone to remember a lone soldier had ridden recently from Metz, Egar avoided the main roads. He had to return to Paris before he was missed in the palace. He tried to spirit himself home using magic—to no avail.

Chapter Twenty-Four

Once in Paris, Egar barely managed to tell Pepin all was well, before succumbing to dreamless sleep. He drifted in and out of consciousness for two days, telling Pepin the details in bits and pieces. Finally, late in the third day, he awoke feeling fuzzy-headed. As Pepin was nowhere to be seen, Egar took his cloak from the peg and went out, hoping the cold air would settle his queasiness.

Even in the dead of winter the bailey seemed a busy place. Soldiers walked horses while their stalls were mucked out. People hurried, carrying buckets of water, vegetables from the root cellar, wood for the fires, anxious to be indoors as soon as possible. The activity made Egar's head ache.

Gelasius, well-dressed as usual, separated himself from a group of men. Egar knew the nobleman to be an intimate of Dagobert's—one of his inner council— and thought it strange he should go out of his way to come stand next to one who sat so far down the table as did he and Pepin these days.

"Well met, Egar." The smile on Gelasius' face failed to reach his hazel eyes. "Feel you better?"

Egar was taken aback. He felt wretched. But, to what was Gelasius referring? Better than what?

"Pepin said you were ill nearly a week ago. I can see he spoke but truth." His words lacked compassion. "Perhaps bad meat? A soldier has also been confined to his pallet for several days."

Leave it to the gods, thought Egar, to exact retribution with one hand and give me a plausible alibi with the other.

"I thought the stories swirling about Pepin's family's escape from Metz were far-fetched, but I can see now you were in no shape to actually travel there and back so swiftly as to have done the deed yourself."

Egar caught his breath. "What stories are those?"

"How you put a spell on them and flew them off in the middle of the night on the wings of giant bats." Gelasius' look became cunning. "Your participation through stealth and sorcery reflects service to Pepin in defiance of the king."

"I am a loyal subject, sir. As is Pepin—"

Gelasius payed no heed to Egar's declaration. "I knew you to be a middling juggler and singer, but had no idea you could add sorcery to your list of accomplishments as well!" He looked as if he would love telling Dagobert tales which would put Egar in a bad light—and by so doing, build his own reputation with the king.

Egar shrugged, trying to look innocent of all charges.

Gelasius gave a mocking salute and walked away.

Later that night Pepin and Egar talked in their darkened alcove.

"You hoodwinked them well! Not even Gelasius is sure but what I have been here all along."

"Little difficulty. The court was in an uproar."

"Why is that?"

"The Wends have invaded Francia's border. Dagobert ordered the new mayor in Metz to join their

Neustrian cousins in defense of the kingdom." Pepin sighed, his shoulders sagging. "Yet he will not allow me to lead my army to battle as is my right. I am to remain prisoner here in Paris!"

Pepin sat on the bench, his head in his hands, his shoulders hunched. Egar could think of no way to console him.

At last Pepin raised his head. "Dagobert has heard of your exploit in sending my family to safety and is displeased."

"So Gelasius led me to believe," replied Egar. "I understood the risk when I allowed myself to be seen by the king's messengers. I knew word would be carried back to Dagobert." Egar shrugged, hopelessly. "My hand was forced."

"Be forewarned. Do nothing to further put yourself at risk." Pepin paused. "If you realized the danger, why returned you here? Surely you could have found some safe place to hide."

"My destiny is bound to yours. I am pledged to you as surely as if I had taken an oath. "

Pepin nodded acknowledgement of Egar's declaration of fealty. "Take care. I cannot believe Dagobert, whom we have known since he was a pup, would ever truly plan us harm, but forget not he is now king and can do what he wishes."

"But what of you? Of the two of us, you are the more likely to be in danger."

"Have no fear. I am experienced. I shall do what I must to regain my rightful place beside the king."

Pepin found, as long as he made no attempt to go beyond the wooden palisade of the royal compound, he was free to come and go at will. Though making it a point to talk pleasantly to everyone he met, he felt isolated. Few were left of the followers Dagobert had brought from Metz. The king now surrounded himself with Neustrians.

Pepin became familiar with those who had become Dagobert's closest companions. He hoped they might speak well of him to their monarch.

Unfortunately, Pepin met none who indicated they would be willing to make an effort on his behalf. Instead, he was given the impression they would betray him if that were ever to their advantage.

Messages from Dagobert's troops arrived in Paris. The Wends were winning. Surprisingly, no soldiers came from Austrasia to join the king's army.

Dagobert sent a frantic message to the recently appointed Neustrian mayor of the palace in Metz. "Call all who have pledged themselves to you on my behalf. You must join the battle immediately. Our realm is in grave peril!"

Word arrived by return messenger. "My lord, king, the noblemen refuse to fight for a province you prefer to theirs. In their anger, they willingly commit treason!"

Dagobert finally realized he was likely to lose not only the battle with the Wends, but all of Austrasia as well. He summoned the Austrasian bishops and nobles to a council in Paris.

Chapter Twenty-Five

From all corners of the kingdom seigneurs converged on Paris. Noblemen, mud-spattered and blue-white with cold came to stand close to any fire offering heat. Those of Dagobert's supporters from Neustria and Burgundy who were not at the border fighting, were equally glad to find themselves in the palace, protected from the cold and damp. The delegation from Metz was the last to arrive.

Pepin was pleased when a page came to his chamber. "M'lord Pepin, King Dagobert requests your presence in the deliberations on the morrow."

Pepin walked into the hall, head held high, to take his seat near the foot of the table. He looked toward the throne, thinking with envy of the many times he had sat on the dais next to the king. He was dismayed to see Grimo and Adalgisel among the Austrasians from Metz, seated in positions of prominence near the head of the table. They stared at him with unmasked hostility. Gelasius sat nearby.

All of the men stood when the king strode to his carved chair. They lifted goblets of wine in salute to their monarch and then, ceremoniously drank to his health.

Dagobert addressed the assembly. "Well met, my lords." The king took time to look each delegate in the eye. "I understand those of you from Austrasia feel yourselves too far removed from the royal ear."

The Metz delegation shifted uneasily on their benches.

"As we cannot dwell in Paris and Metz at the same time, we are prepared to offer the same solution as did my father in naming me to the Austrasian throne. I give you my son, Sigibert III, king of Austrasia."

The Austrasians, surprised but pleased, were undaunted by the king's tender age, a bare three years. It was enough he was a Merovingian and their own. It seemed fitting that Sigibert—whose mother, Gomatrud, was locked away in a convent—should be king of Austrasia where he was born. His hair would grow long and the palace would once again become a royal residence. Even better, the power would stay where it belonged, in their own capable hands.

"As Sigibert is yet a child," said Dagobert, "and unable to rule without the help of trusted advisors, I am appointing Chunibert, Bishop of Metz, as special advisor to the throne. I have also decided, in recognition of the strong ties you have with leaders chosen from within your own ranks, to name an Austrasian as mayor of the palace."

Had you asked, Pepin thought, I could have told you naming a Neustrian mayor was a grave mistake. He could hardly contain the sudden rush of gratitude that swept over him. His hours of quiet diplomacy were about to bear fruit. Dagobert's advisors, whom he had carefully courted, must have convinced the king he posed no threat to the crown. He was going to be reinstated as mayor of the palace! He was going home. He would once again be in a position of authority. He was...

"*Duke Adalgisel* will be your new mayor of the palace!"

Adalgisel shot Pepin a killing look of triumph. Their eyes locked. Adalgisel's spewed hatred while Pepin sent a look, cold with contempt. Adalgisel looked away first—but with a gloating expression of victory.

Pepin noted conspiratorial gestures of congratulation between Gelasius, Adalgisel and Grimo. Gelasius was the source of Pepin's lack of favor with the king! The Gallo-Roman would do anything to promote himself at the expense of those nearby who might earn the king's blessing.

For the first time, Pepin felt fear. Before, he had been angry but never afraid. His heart beat with quickened irregularity. Not merely his position, now his *life* was seriously threatened.

It galled Pepin to think power he had worked so hard to attain had fallen into the hands of the Grimo-Adalgisel family. They were in an unassailable position to eliminate any threat he might once have posed.

The only reason he had been invited to attend the council was for Dagobert to publicly humiliate him. The king wanted him to witness his own replacement by a man who had been his rival for years.

Pepin felt his face flush. He looked at the bland features of fleshy Dagobert and was met by a look of indifference. Had he stood and shouted to the assembled, "Never again will Pepin the Vain look on me as if I were still the ignorant young student and he the superior tutor," Dagobert could not have been more plain.

Knowing every eye was on him, Pepin dared not look around the table. He tried to match Dagobert's look with his own mask of detachment. His mind was spinning. To whom could he turn?

Bishop Chunibert might once have favored him. But with his appointment as special advisor to Sigibert added to the fact Dagobert had made him Bishop of

Metz, there seemed little likelihood Chunibert would risk the king's displeasure.

The Austrasian delegation smiled happily. They pledged again to become warriors for the crown. They would lead their troops to fight alongside the Neustrians and help defeat the Wends. Completely satisfied with the king's decision, Pepin knew he had no allies among them. His cause seemed irrevocably lost.

The representatives from Neustria and Burgundy stood.

"Now that Metz has its own king, Austrasia will once again become overly powerful," a delegate from Soissons complained.

"What will become of us?" cried a nobleman wearing the insignia of Burgundy.

"If you die, will Sigibert become king of both Austrasia and Neustria?" asked a seigneur from Paris.

"How will we defend ourselves against Austrasia's strength?" queried another.

"Upon my death," Dagobert pledged, "you shall have my child by Queen Nanthild, Clovis II, as king of Neustria and Burgundy. While I have ample heirs, you shall have a king of your own."

Pepin sat very still, as if he could stop the rapid beating of his heart by willing it so. He watched Dagobert savor his council's response. With the Austrasians firmly behind him, Pepin knew the king was assured victory over the Wends. And by naming Adalgisel he has demolished me. I wonder if he will seek to have me killed. What pleasure it must give him to have Pepin the Vain completely in his power.

As soon as the council was dismissed Pepin left for his own quarters where Egar awaited news.

Egar heard the report with growing alarm.

"*Your* prophecy caused this!" Pepin hissed. "I was content to be chosen tutor to the prince. Had you not tempted me with promise of the crown, I would have been overjoyed as mayor of the palace in Metz. But no, you guaranteed my future as the greatest king of all time and my desire knew no bounds.

"And now I am nothing. No longer mayor of the palace. Forbidden to lead my troops to war. I cannot even come and go as I wish."

"I never *promised* you would be king. I saw not the face clearly—"

"I know that!" Pepin's voice, though quiet, had the force to stop Egar in mid-sentence. "But *your* vision led to my being prisoner. It put my family in danger. I *wish* we had never met!"

Both men recoiled in shocked silence from words that once uttered could never be recalled.

"I did not mean that as it sounded," Pepin said. "But my life would have been much simpler had I not wanted so desperately to believe you."

"I do understand." Egar replied.

"I owe you a great debt," continued Pepin, "for risking your life to assure my family's safety. I cannot live with that unpaid on my conscience. I know not what Dagobert intends for me but I no longer have the power to protect you."

"Surely he means you no physical harm?" asked Egar.

"There is no guarantee of that, nor of your own safety. You must leave. Immediately. The palace. Paris. Once gone, never return."

Egar had never seen Pepin frightened before. He was alarmed both for himself and his friend.

"Remember," continued Pepin, "what his father did to Brundhilde. Think what kind of magician, juggler and singer of ballads you will be if the king orders your hands cut off, your tongue cut out!"

Egar gagged at the image.

To live is to be at risk. The long-ago voice of his Master echoed in his head. *There are many kinds of danger and many kinds of pain. In your long life you will experience your share of both.*

Egar ran his fingers through his hair, his palms suddenly sweaty. "But what will happen to you, alone in the palace, held prisoner by the king?"

Pepin sighed. "I shall do what I must to survive. But I will not have you on my conscience. Now get out—before I change my mind and selfishly wish you back!"

Chapter Twenty-Six

Egar snatched his traveling cloak and bag from the pegs beside the doorway and left the room. Fear and anger rose in equal portions. Pepin's outburst, though immediately rescinded, spoke of his true feelings.

It is not my fault, Egar fumed. I never promised he would be king. Only that I saw the vision when I looked at him. That he lusted for the throne is his business, not mine.

Egar stopped. His body froze. Early dusk had fallen and the torches in the gallery were lit. In the flickering light he saw a guard sitting on a low stool beside the doorway to their room. Had the king already posted a watchman? Fortunately the guard was turned away, sharpening his knife and humming tunelessly to himself.

Egar pressed back into the deeply set doorway, thankful his moss-colored cloak blended into the shadows. The guard stopped humming. Egar's heart thumped. Had he heard the movement of the leather curtain?

The guard resumed his humming.

Egar felt as though he were the prey, with one foot already caught in the snare. How can I leave the palace? He concentrated his senses on the sights and sounds of the hallway. The rhythmic rubbing of the guard's knife against the whet-stone accompanied the tune he hummed. The torch crackled as it burned, providing as much smoke as light. The wintry drafts pushed the flame this way and that.

Egar matched his powers to the errant wind currents swirling about the gallery. He encompassed the cold draft chilling his feet and with an effort lifted it higher, bending it, making it stronger. Another gust gathered outside in the dark. As the wind blew in along the open passageway, Egar with a surge of effort, pulled it higher and higher yet. With all his might, he threw it at the burning torch. It flared, showing Egar plainly in the brilliant light, then was just as suddenly extinguished in a cloud of smoke.

"By the...!" exclaimed the guard looking up from his knife. Slowly he rose and took down the smoldering, blackened torch. He turned to re-light it from another which still burned steadily a ways down the gallery. In the few moments this took, Egar left, swiftly blending into the darkness.

He pulled open the stable door. It protested with a heart-stopping screech. Egar expected to feel a guard's hand on his shoulder at any moment, his flight stopped before it had begun. No one stirred and his heart resumed its normal pace. He would take his own horse, the splotchy grey Pepin had given him.

The stable was nearly empty. Most of the soldiers and their mounts had left for the fighting on the eastern border. Egar made his way stealthily to the last stall where his horse nickered in greeting to be answered by another several stalls away.

"My good friend, Egar!" The voice was smooth with malice.

Egar spun around. Gelasius was but a dark shape silhouetted in the doorway.

"So *that* is how you warned Pepin's family! By sneaking off like a thief in the night. And where might you be going this time?"

Egar stepped away from his horse. "Why care you what I do?"

"I care about anyone whose activities might affect the king."

Self-righteous prick! thought Egar, surprised. He seldom felt loathing for anyone—and he hardly knew the man.

"Pepin is well out of it," Gelasius continued, "but you concern me. Not that I grant you a sorcerer's power! Nonetheless, you are an enigma. Pepin's harmless young companion? I think not. He treats you with uncommon respect for someone of your tender years.

"When I saw you slip out the great hall I wondered what sinister errand might occupy your night. So, tell me, what mischief are you up to?"

Egar tried to still the pounding of his heart. "Nothing to concern you, Gelasius."

"*Everything* you do concerns me!"

A knife appeared in Gelasius' hand, gleaming dully in the fitful moon glow. He took a step closer to Egar. "Perhaps this will convince you to tell me what you are about."

"Nothing devious. Pepin is upset with me and has cast me out."

"God's death! You expect me to believe that? And you thick as thieves. Tell me your plot or I shall stop it aborning with a knife stab to your gut."

Egar's knees turned to jelly.

"Tell or fight," taunted Gelasius drawing nearer yet. Suddenly the stable seemed much too small. And darker than midnight as the moon went once more behind a cloud.

"I have nothing to tell and no wish to fight."

"Then I shall kill you without a fight."

Gelasius stepped ever closer. Egar could smell him —a not unpleasant combination of onions and musk. Egar dropped his travel bag in a corner. Allowed his cloak to slip off and fall on top of it. Somehow his hunting knife was in his hand, though he had no recollection of unsheathing it. Until now its use had been confined to cutting and spearing meat at table.

"I have no training in warfare," Egar said.

"By the three! A young man of the court not taught to fight? That is more farfetched than your last lie."

Egar backed up a step and felt the prickling sensation of a wall close behind him. He need not reach out to feel there was no maneuvering room in that direction. He gestured to the right as he moved to the left.

Gelasius grunted as he stabbed air. "And you claim no training! God's blood, I shall see you feel pain before I put you out of your lying, scheming misery."

No lie, thought Egar. Merely a magician's skill to direct the onlooker's eye away from the action.

The knife came within a hairsbreadth of his neck and he could hear Gelasius breathing hard. Without thought Egar spun away again with a juggler's nimbleness. In an instant Gelasius was on him again.

I can duck and dodge forever, Egar thought, and Gelasius will keep coming. I know not how to stab a man and doubt I could do it if I did. Egar pushed forward. Moved backward. Sidestepped slightly—to see what Gelasius would do.

The nobleman committed himself to a forward thrust. Realizing his mistake, he tried to change direction. As he did so, his foot caught in Egar's fallen cloak. Gelasius twisted and tripped. Crashing into Egar.

In an instant Gelasius' weight pinned Egar to the floor, the wind knocked painfully out of him. He felt a quick sting where Gelasius' knife nicked him under the chin. But far worse was the agonizing ache of his wrist. In falling, the man had somehow snagged himself on

Egar's knife and twisted the wrist with his full weight on top of it.

Egar frantically shoved Gelasius off, wondering at the same time, how to defend himself. His now useless hand came up empty. He struggled to his knees. Waited, panting, for the nobleman to renew his fatal attack.

Gelasius rolled over.

Why so still? Egar reached and felt a flaccid arm. Searching further with his fingers in the darkness, he found his knife. The handle protruded from Gelasius' gut, the point buried deep under his ribcage.

Egar felt frantically for a pulse, a breath, any sign of life. None.

His legs gave way, dumping him with a hard thump on the dirt floor. Uncontrollable shivering washed over him. Cold burrowed deep within his bones. His teeth chattered violently in his mouth.

Egar tried to marshall his senses. It had been kill or be killed. The thought gave no comfort.

He pulled his knees up. Wrapped his arms tightly around them. The shaking continued, unabated.

What to do now?

Get out!

But, the... Egar swallowed as vomit surged, subsided. The *body*. He could not leave it here. What if someone should come?

He crawled unsteadily to the last stall. Pulled himself to his feet. Grabbed his horse's rope halter. The horse shied as it pranced delicately around Gelasius' body.

Egar swallowed, feeling sick again.

He tied the horse, then dragged Gelasius to the empty stall. Covered him with straw.

He retrieved his travel bag and cloak. Started to mount, then thought, what if someone comes looking for Gelasius and finds him in my horse's empty stall? They will know I am the killer—the murderer. At the realization, Egar lost control and vomited in the corner of the stable.

The trembling began again. They will find me, drag me to face Dagobert. The punishment for killing a nobleman... He could not complete the thought.

The gate to the bridge off the island was closed and barred for the night. He must delay a mounted search until he had a chance to escape. But how?

He mopped his brow. His knees stopped shaking.

A plan slowly formed.

Egar gathered the half dozen horses remaining in the stable building. Cautiously, he led them out into the night and through the shadows. Across the bailey. Holding his breath at every wind-driven shadow. Through the little-used and unguarded back gate. Once outside, he took time to spirit the bolt back into place.

Egar mounted his own horse, driving the others before him. Once again, he had escaped the palace. With luck, he would never see it again.

The sound of hooves hitting the street's paving stones echoed loudly. Egar held his breath, then sighed with relief as no one opened their shuttered windows to see who was riding through the dark night. Allowing the other horses to wander off at will, Egar looked for a haystack to shelter him until the city gate opened at daybreak.

Chapter Twenty-Seven

Egar awoke to swirling fog, his body stiff and chilled. He crawled out, brushing at bits of straw that stuck to his clothing. His bound wrist throbbed. Though swollen and painful, Egar was thankful it was not broken.

He joined the small cluster of people waiting for the city gate to open. They stood, a silent, half asleep group—peasants going into the forest to find wood for the fire, a family on the road, a man, his mule laden with peddler's supplies.

Egar shivered in fear. He dared not look the guard full in the face. Was he even now searching the indistinct faces waiting in the mist, hoping to drag to court someone who had murdered a nobleman?

At last the guard slid the heavy bolt and the tall wooden gate creaked open. Heart in his mouth, head down, eyes darting from side to side, Egar saw nothing but mud and a sea of legs walking in the same direction as he.

He half expected to hear the guard call out, "You there! Where do you think you are going?" Egar's legs threatened to buckle once more. He could almost feel the hand clamped on the back of his neck as the guard barked, "You are wanted for the murder of nobleman Gelasius!"

No one paid him any mind as the group crossed the bridge and began to disperse.

At last daring to mount, Egar rode alone into the forest, his mind a jumbled swirl of unfinished thoughts.

His spirits lifted as they always did when he left the confines of the palace for the untrammeled woods. A sense of relief filled him as he finally acknowledged he had slipped away unnoticed. At the same time, he experienced an unexpected emptiness. Not only had he killed a man, he had run to save his own life, leaving Pepin to fend as best he could.

Egar shivered. Pulling his cloak more tightly about him, he urged the horse farther into the thick woods where snow lay in patches under the sun's weak rays.

He rode toward the sanctuary of his remembered cave. There he might have time to figure out what to do next. The path, overgrown with vines and at one point blocked by a fallen tree, was harder to follow than he recalled. Could it truly have been nine years since he left Paris with the young Dagobert about to be crowned king?

Just when he was about to give up and turn back, Egar found the cave. By nightfall he had cleared it of debris and prepared to start a fire at the entrance. It seemed harder than usual to gather his wits. Egar took a deep breath and summoned all the energy he could muster. He thought darkly of his failure to start the fire after being sent away from Stonehenge.

Taking no chances, he used both hands to consolidate his power as he directed flame to the nest of moss and dried leaves. For a moment he was afraid he was doomed once more to failure. Then an almost imperceptable spot of red began to glow and a minute thread of smoke curled upward. Encouraged by his success, Egar pushed his power with renewed vigor and soon a sturdy flame licked at the twigs.

Enjoying the sensation of warmth on his face, Egar pondered what had just occurred. The gift of magic seemed irrevocably related to his own feeling of confidence. It was a concept he would do well to remember.

As long as he was actively engaged, Egar was able to keep his troubled thoughts at bay, though they clawed and snapped at him like hunting dogs around a cornered animal. Now, in the quiet of the cave, he could no longer fend them off.

With a shudder, he relived the previous night—the stable, Gelasius, feinting, followed by the crashing fall. Nausea threatened to overcome him at the memory of his own knife handle, protruding from Gelasius, covered in warm, sticky blood.

I killed him, Egar admitted. It was no murder, but I *did* kill him. That he attacked first matters little. He is... was... a nobleman, and I an itinerant entertainer.

A thought took hold which stunned him to his toes. He could *never* return to the Frankish court! Pepin, held prisoner, could not leave it. *In this one rash act of violence, he had severed all connection to his god-endowed destiny.*

Heart pounding in his chest, Egar sought direction in the flames and smoke. He searched for reassurance in his Master's face. Nothing. The fire's warmth offered solace—but no guidance.

With a heavy sigh, Egar took stock of his situation. He had the clothes on his back, all of them ordinary garments, his old moss-colored travel cloak, and a change of tunics, underdrawers and wool stockings in his travel bag.

He had the horse Pepin had given him three years before, a somewhat plodding animal of an unusual mottled grey color. Egar thought his horse's unique coloring resembled the smoke that rose from his fire. He decided to call the animal Smoke. Once named, it would be almost like having a friend.

He had the blanket now spread as his bed, a few coins which he had earned long ago and some medicines of his own devising which he kept in the bottom of his travel bag—camomile to induce the devil out of the digestive tract, willow bark which eased pain, mustard seed for pastes and poultices, salves and lotions of alkonet, anemone, mint and figwort.

Egar wondered what he should do next. He could, if necessary, live off the land here in the forest until next winter. But it was probably unwise to remain so close to Paris. He wondered if Dagobert had already given an order to find and return him to the royal residence. If so, any soldier would be elated to capture Egar and win the prize.

He could not go to Metz.

Should he go to Pepin's family estates in Landen? Would they help him, or call him murderer and turn him in, themselves?

Egar thought not. But that would be the first place Dagobert's guard might look for him. In addition to placing himself in danger, his presence might also put Itta and Bega at risk. They were safe there only so long as no one drew unnecessary attention to them.

I must leave Neustria. I could travel north and east to Austrasia, keeping well away from Metz. At least there I know the land. I will have to be alert for any hint soldiers are searching for me. If I start out at dawn I should be away from the area of immediate danger in a day or two.

Egar started early, working his way northward. He fretted about earning his keep. He dared not gain food and a pallet, as he once had, with simple magic, juggling and singing. Someone might put these skills together with a missing court entertainer and haul him, bound and gagged, back to Paris.

Emerging from the forest he met a farmer driving a slow, creaking wagon. Its solid wooden wheels protested with every turn. The poor ox barely managed to drag its noisome burden.

"God's greeting," Egar said as cheerfully as possible.

"By the dog, I have seen better," responded the farmer morosely.

"Oh, it is hard times these be," agreed Egar equably.

"God's death, they be..."

Over the screech of the wagon wheels Egar became acutely aware of pounding hooves on the road behind them. Too far away yet to be heard by his outer ear, nevertheless he knew in a flash of intuition that the cadence came from several horses, maintaining a well-disciplined canter. A contingent of soldiers rode toward him. Palace guards? At their distance-eating pace it would be no time at all before they overtook the slowly moving cart.

Egar looked around for some means of escape or cover. None. Pitifully few bags of newly milled flour nowhere near filled the wagon. No hiding place there. The road gave onto the river on one side, dense forest on the other. If he were to suddenly run away, crashing into the trees, the farmer would certainly send the soldiers chasing after him.

Frantically Egar tried to think of magic that might save him from capture. Nothing that would not at the same time startle the farmer into betraying him. Becoming more and more anxious, Egar remembered how his gifts failed him when he lacked confidence.

"This be the last of the grain for flour 'till after next fall's harvest," continued the farmer, droning on above the sound of his wagon, unaware of the approaching soldiers. "And if the summer be a rainy one..."

Egar felt the sweat begin to trickle down his forehead and dampen the pits of his arms.

"And our cow be standing on three legs for near a week now. I figure she's got foul..."

Egar strained to hear the farmer over the squeal of wooden wheels. His own heart pounded nearly as loudly, driven by the rhythm of the horses' hooves inexorably gaining on them. Egar strained to understand the dialect the farmer spoke.

"... by the smell of it, it be foul, sure enough..."

"Freeman," Egar shouted to the farmer, "I have some skill at curing. Where is this cow of yours? Perhaps I could..."

But it was already too late, the sound of the soldiers' horses was clearly audible now. Soon the men would be within sight of Egar and the cart.

"It be just off the road here. Our farm be in a clearing in the woods."

At the farmer's motion, Egar turned Smoke onto a narrow lane cut through the thickly growing foliage. The farmer forced the ox and wagon to turn onto the track behind him.

The troops swept by neither slowing nor turning. Egar chanced a quick glance over his shoulder, beyond the wagon. He had been right. It was a party of the king's own guard from Paris. He recognized the faces of the two men nearest him as they rode intently onward. Had they ridden past him on the road, they could not have helped but see him. Would certainly have recognized him.

It was miraculous the narrow track led off when it did. That he had met the farmer to show him the way at the very moment it was most needed. Miraculous? Or the work of the gods? Perhaps they had plans for him yet.

Chapter Twenty-Eight

The cow had foul of the foot, so named for the stinking dead tissue between the cleats. Egar had never treated a large animal before, but he could see what was needed. Wrestling with the lunging hind foot, Egar dressed the infected cleft with a mixture of powdered blue crystals of copper salts and tar, finishing with a pad of cotton wool held by a tight bandage.

"By the dog, ye do be having the healing touch," the farmer exclaimed. "That be a right proper job ye did. We have naught to pay ye, but by the light, ye'll stay for a well-deserved supper and bed down for the night."

The farmer's hut, made of wattle and daub, was cramped and dirty, the earthen floor uncovered by reeds. It evoked a far-off memory of the home Egar had left when he climbed the hill to the Old Master. I have lived too long in court, he thought. It is good to spend time in more humble dwellings else I come to disdain honest folk who live here. That they live in such squalid conditions is not to be held against them. They know no better. Have small choice.

The potage, a soup the consistency of mush, containing mashed vegetables and a few small dabs of smoked pork, was ladled into a hollowed loaf of extremely hard, stale bread. As Egar ate hungrily, the potage softened the bread and made it chewable. With it they drank fresh milk from the cow he had so recently treated.

Egar's pallet on the floor was not too different from his bed in the cave. He dreamt of soldiers pounding after him to the thundering of his own heartbeat. He could not escape. In the darkness the horses drew closer and closer.

Suddenly he was a small boy and he saw a figure of a woman ahead. He could not make out the features but he knew instinctively it was his mother. She held out her arms in love and welcome. He wanted, needed, to feel the security of those arms as he had needed little else in his life. He strove desperately to achieve shelter there but, try as he might, could move no closer. The thundering was overtaking him. He was helpless to save himself.

Waking with pounding heart, Egar knew the dream was not a message from the gods but a reflection of his scrambled state of mind.

At least he knew how he could earn his way. He would stay at humble farms and inconspicuous huts. The people there always had need of healing for themselves or their animals. They could not pay him, of course, but they could shelter and feed him. His needs were simple. He would travel slowly, gathering the herbs, roots and molds necessary for concocting his medicines. It was the perfect disguise for a court entertainer running for his life.

Keeping to little used roads and forest tracks, Egar made his way northward. Arriving at a cluster of thatch-roofed buildings, he would stop at the least prosperous. Here he asked directions to the nearest town, or struck up a conversation about the weather, keeping his eyes and ears open. Usually he found someone with a racking cough, or an open sore oozing puss. Generously he administered something from his bag of healing salves and potions and then, in gratitude, was offered a bed and meal for his trouble.

One evening Egar found himself in a small, smoke-filled hovel. He was sharing supper with the family when the door opened.

Rigunth, the eldest daughter, entered and wearily sat on a stool. "They be king's soldiers at the inn tonight."

Egar froze, his spoon half-way to his mouth.

"That be why it took me so long when I be taking our eggs," she continued. "They was all running this way and that at the soldier's orders. 'Bring more ale. We need fresh bread. What! No roast on the spit?' I never did hear so many orders all at the very same time!

"Innkeeper finally took our eggs but he be having no bread for us in trade. Them soldiers ate everything in sight. He say he give us bread when them soldiers be moving on."

"Why be they here?" Her father's voice rose with apprehension. "It be not time to collect the king's share of harvest and we be not at war. Why else come they to our poor corner of Dagobert's realm?"

"They be looking for a powerful sorcerer on a grey horse that have killed a nobleman then run away from the king's court," Rigunth replied.

Egar choked on the soup he had managed to spoon into his mouth.

"Most horses be brown," mused the farmer, "or maybe black or white if they be the king's, but there be no grey horses..."

Egar held his breath, trying not to sputter on the soup caught in his throat.

"*Your* horse be gray, be it not?" asked the farmer turning to Egar.

Egar coughed. "There are many such where I come from." He stared into the wooden trencher in front of him. His mind conjured up a picture of a guard's rough hand on his neck, dragging him back to court, a prisoner.

"Skilled as ye be at healing," continued the farmer, "ye be no powerful sorcerer." Egar breathed a sigh of relief. "No man with magical power ever be coming among us here."

Egar found it suddenly hard to breathe, as if the stench and smoke were about to stifle him. I must be off, he thought, as the conversation wound around him. I would leave tonight if it would not make the family suspicious. Tomorrow early, I will be away.

One of these days someone will recognize Smoke by her unusual coloring and then my life will be at risk. Was there some way to disguise his horse's coloring? He could think of no dye that would look natural yet withstand Smoke's sweat and the effects of frequent rain. Where could he go?

He thought of his own family who lived at the far eastern boundary of Austrasia. Ostensibly under Sigibert's rule, Dagobert's soldiers could still follow him there. However, no one at court knew where he came from or who his family was. They would not think to look for him there. Going home would pose no danger to either his parents or himself.

On the small farm which his father worked as tenant, far from the glitter and controversy of court, no one would ever have heard of Egar, king's magician and singer of ballads. Returning home would be very like going back into another world.

What kind of reception might he expect after so many years? It was entirely possible their seeming lack of love and affection for him was only in his mind or caused by some juvenile misbehavior on his part. Surely when he returned, a man fully grown, they would greet him with warmth.

He should see them while he still could. His mother and father would be old by now, his brother and sister grown with families of their own.

He was only sorry he would be arriving in such modest circumstances. He should be wearing his court tunics, his magic robe of black and gold, have his traveling harp, his magical paraphernalia. To make them proud of him. To earn their love.

Chapter Twenty-Nine

The roads, mired in mud, were saturated by spring rains. Egar could hardly remember a time when he had been warm or dry. He slept poorly, hearing in his dreams the soldiers' horses riding after him.

Drawing closer to his parent's home, his heart lifted. He came to the narrow dirt track that led through scraggly fields to the hut with its pig sty and the necessary behind. Although full daylight, there seemed to be no one about. No tell-tale wisp of smoke came from the hole in the roof. Then he saw figures in a field off in the distance. Behind them the forest seemed black and menacing.

As Egar approached he could see his brother, full-grown as he knew he would be, harnessed to a wooden plow while his father, bent nearly double with age, guided the point to make a shallow furrow. Following him, a strange woman—Egar guessed her to be his brother's wife—sowed seeds while three small children gathered stones to carry to the walls growing at the edge of the field.

Egar rode forward.

The figures stopped in their tracks, staring at him.

"Do you not know me?" he asked as he drew up to them. "Father, it is me, Egar. Do you remember me, Ogier, my brother?"

His brother straightened. He shaded his eyes with his hands. His eyes were wide, his mouth a round "O" of surprise. "Be that truly you, Egar?"

"We thought ye be dead all these years past." His father's hands dangled at his sides. He made no move to come closer, to embrace or even touch him. His dazed face seemed incapable of expressing emotion—surprise, joy, sorrow, anger—any of them.

"Be ye truly me brother?" Ogier asked again, as if he were simple minded.

"Why came ye back?" asked his father.

"I was passing by and thought I would stop for a short visit," Egar replied. "How are you?"

"We be well enough," his father replied.

"As long as I am here, let me help. We can hitch the plow to my horse. It should save you some grief, Ogier. You can both rest a bit and let me guide the plow."

"Ye be not sounding like our Egar," said his father. "Ye speak too fine to be our Egar."

"That is because I have traveled far and wide since I left as a lad. But I have never forgotten any of you. I have longed to return. To see how you fare. To let you know..." What? "...I am alive."

Ogier at last, almost against his will, took Egar by the arm. At the touch, their eyes locked and Egar felt a thrill as recognition lit his brother's face.

"Do let me help," Egar said again.

They seemed uncertain about letting him summarily take over the task, but willing enough to rest. With the horse setting the pace, the plowing went faster but the furrows were not as straight as his father's had been.

Egar stopped working, his heart hammering in dread as he saw, off in the distance, a small contingent of soldiers riding briskly down the road he had traveled just that day. He could not breathe until they sped past the narrow track leading to his family's hut. The soldiers had not so much as glanced in their direction. Perhaps he would be safe here, at least for a time. Surely the search for him would not last forever.

Egar spent the rest of the afternoon plowing the field in silence while his father and brother joined the children carrying rocks to clear the ground. At last it grew too dark to see. The warm welcome he had anticipated never came, but Egar felt gratified to be of assistance.

As they trudged back to the hut the children clustered curiously about Egar's horse. Neither they nor Ogier's wife had said a word in greeting.

On entering the two-room villein's hut, the smell of filth assaulted Egar's nostrils. Memories flooded back. The home of his birth. Dark. Dirty. Earthen floor unswept, hardly even packed.

Ogier's wife started a smoldering fire on a stone slab in the center of the floor. Most of the smoke drifted about the room, making their eyes water. A few wisps finally escaped through the hole cut in the thatched roof. Tools hung on the walls. A string of onions and some herbs but no strips of dried meat dangled from the rafters.

Egar heard the sound of a racking cough and a low moan from the adjoining room. He crossed quickly to the low doorway and ducked under. His mother lay on a dirty pallet. Her body had wasted away. Her feverish eyes, sunken in a death's mask, held no glimmer of recognition. Only fever and pain.

The children hung back, suddenly bashful. Ogier and his father paid not the slightest attention to the obviously dying woman. Ogier's wife made no attempt to clean her, but did at least offer a cup of water to the parched lips.

Looking about, Egar was glad he had not arrived on a sleek war mount dressed in magical clothes. There was little enough to connect him to this rude and ignorant family. Had he been as splendid as he wished, there would have been no way to bridge the gap that separated them. At least now he had a chance, slim though it was, to draw his family closer.

Without a word he fetched a few dried branches and made a fire that radiated warmth rather than mere smoke. Then he filled a container with water, heating it on the flame. He undressed his mother's unresisting form and tenderly bathed her. Clothed her in his only spare undertunic.

All the while his father and brother sat in an exhausted stupor waiting for Ogier's wife to make them something to eat. The children, having grown bored watching Egar ministering to his mother, scrabbled and fought amid the garbage on the floor like wild dogs over some scrap one of them had found.

Egar searched his bag and brought out a packet of powder to ease his mother's pain. Nothing in his pharmacopoeia could cure her. He mixed the powder into a small portion of the potage his sister-in-law had heated over the fire. Holding his mother, he gently spooned tiny bits of the mixture into her mouth. She stared at him with blank eyes.

Egar experienced a wonderful sense of satisfaction watching the gradual change in her. As her pain lessened she became aware of her surroundings. At first she stretched out her hands, the knuckles swollen with age and hard work. She felt the clean tunic, touched her freshly-washed face in something like wonder. She turned her clearing eyes to Egar's face, giving the first small indication she recognized him. A smile began to work on her wrinkled lips, showing gaps where teeth had fallen out.

Egar's chest swelled with pride and love. He was happy he had decided to return home. He was in time to help ease his mother's pain, make her last days as clean and comfortable as possible. He could spend some time here. Perhaps a month or two, until the king's soldiers no longer hunted him.

Suddenly his mother's smile turned into a grimace. She looked at him in horror. Her high-pitched shriek cut into Egar. "Ye! Ye are to blame! Get out. Go back where ye came from."

"What are you talking about?" He took her into his arms and gently stroked her face. "Mother it is I, Egar. Do you remember me?"

"I should not have brung ye into this house. Go away. Leave us be. Leave me die in peace."

Egar could not believe his eyes or ears. Bewildered, he staggered from the room, picked up his belongings and bundled them onto his horse. His father and brother watched as if he were a total stranger. They spoke not a word. Showed no interest. Made no indication they wished him to remain.

Egar could not begin to guess what had caused his mother's raving. What had he done to warrant this reaction? Clearly his staying would not ease her last days.

With tears brimming in his eyes, he mounted his horse and rode away from a family that seemed unable to offer him love.

Chapter Thirty

Egar rode slowly into a night as dark as his spirits. He could not understand his mother's reaction to him. He had made her feel more comfortable. Why the fear and hate? He shivered and felt his heart drop like a cold stone.

Perhaps she was out of her mind with pain and illness but somehow he could not quite believe it. She had known him just an instant before she cried out. Of that Egar felt certain.

Why did no one urge him to stay? It was as if, in their minds at least, he no longer existed. He thought back to the previous time he had left his family.

At the age of six or seven, he could not remember now how it came about that he left—simply walked away. Neither his parents nor siblings called him back. If he could recall any emotion from that long ago time, it was a feeling of incredible lightness as if he could float with relief. In contrast, he now felt heavy and sad.

Suddenly his horse stopped, ears quivering. Egar listened intently. The night was calm. The horse shied as the sound of a faint cry came from somewhere deep in the forest. Was it an animal? Some nocturnal cat?

There it was again, hauntingly like the wail of a human baby.

Egar turned the horse into the forest, moving toward the sound. The horse reluctantly obeyed, its mottled grey coat blending into the shadows. Egar remembered the trials he had endured because his curiosity led him into places he should have avoided. He fervently hoped he was not about to make the same mistake again.

They made slow progress, stopping every few moments to wait and listen for the sound. The more he heard it, the more convinced Egar became it was the wail of an infant, though why it was crying late at night in the middle of the forest was more than he could fathom.

Gradually the cries drew nearer until Egar arrived at a clearing in a grove of evergreens. In the middle stood a giant ash tree, next to it a pile of stones. The area was completely silent... and empty.

Gradually the sounds of crickets and other night insects filled the air. Even Smoke stood for a few moments and then, relaxing, began to graze.

Egar looked about in wonder. Although the grove of trees was nearly black, the ash shone with a silvery radiance and the stones were clearly visible. All at once Egar knew where he was. Gellert's tomb!

He walked over to touch the stones, remembering as he did so the tale his Old Master had told him...

Long, long ago, before the coming of the Romans, when Odin and Thor ruled the forests, lived a warrior named Hilderic. His wife had died in childbirth, leaving him but two beings whom he loved more than life itself, his infant son and his wolfhound, Gellert.

One day Hilderic went hunting, leaving Gellert to guard his baby son asleep in its cradle. At the end of the day he returned to see the overturned cradle, Gellert next to it, his muzzle and paws covered in blood.

With a cry of anguish and rage, Hilderic pulled his hunting knife from its sheath and killed the unsuspecting dog. Then with an angry jerk, he pulled the cradle upright and beheld his infant son, tears still drying on his cheeks, but alive and peacefully sleeping. Next to the child lay a pile of rough and matted fur, the dead carcass of a wild wolf.

At once Hilderic knew the whole story and realized in his grief he had committed a terrible injustice. While he was off hunting, the hungry wolf had slunk out of the forest. Gellert, true to his duty to guard the baby, courageously fought the wolf. Emerging victorious he continued to lie close by to protect the child as it cried itself to sleep.

Hilderic's heart twisted inside his chest as he beheld the once beautiful dog, now dead. If only he could take back that one awful act!

With tear-filled eyes, he picked up the lifeless body of his faithful friend and gently carried it to his favorite place in the forest. There, next to a giant ash tree, sacred to Odin, Hilderic buried the dog, placing stones on top of the grave to keep predators from digging up the body.

Hilderic moved away and little by little, the forest reclaimed the spot where his home had once stood. At the same time, people began adding stones to Gellert's grave, building a cairn to the one who had so courageously protected the infant in his charge. As the years passed, the forest people began to pray to Gellert, protector of Hilderic's son, to guard over their own small children. When they converted to Christianity, the Catholic Church added to its pantheon of saints, one called Gellert. Only a very few people, living deep in the forest, far from the village priests and bishops, knew that Saint Gellert had once been, not a man, but a dog.

Egar looked down, touching the stones of Gellert's grave. He was no longer apprehensive. Wrapping himself in his blanket, he lay at the foot of the tree growing next to the cairn. Egar slept and while sleeping dreamed...

A woman approached the grave, a small baby wrapped in a blanket in her arms. It was too dark to see her clearly but he had seen her before.

Fearfully, the woman handed the baby to an old crone who appeared from nowhere. Bent over, she supported herself with a walking stick. Grey hair hung lank and tangled, framing an ugly face. Wearing a shapeless black garment, she reached for the baby with gnarled fingers. She smiled crookedly, gaps appearing where teeth were missing.

The mother of the babe was clearly frightened, though emboldened by her plight. Her infant was sick and near death.

"Go," said the witch, taking the child. She unwrapped the blanket and wound a wide red belt around his naked body.

Gathering her powers, she stood quite still before the tree. She passed the baby through a hole in the ash and began to sing.

> *This is the cleft ash,*
> *It prevails over loathly things.*
> *Flee thee, child sickness less and greater,*
> *Greater and less, I say flee from the child.*
> *You are old, ash tree, give of your wisdom,*
> *At the call of the ash tree, come, you wood*
> *   demons,*
> *Take back your sick child;*
> *bring back our baby, fat and well.*

By the time she finished singing the song, the witch had threaded the baby through the cleft in the ash nine times. She stood silently once more, holding the infant above her head. Finally she placed it in a straw cradle at the foot of the tree.

The silence which followed these weird acts was suddenly rent as the witch let out a blood-chilling scream and jumped up, flinging her arms and legs in a wild dance. Nine times she did this, with an energy that was hard to credit to so old a hag. This finished, she spun round and round, also nine times, like an evil spirit.

Abruptly she vanished into the blackness of the forest.

Egar awoke early the next morning feeling strangely tired, his eyes scratchy, his mouth sour. As he sat up, a sudden wave of dizziness overcame him. His head throbbed with a dull ache. Out of the mists of his discomfort, he remembered the strangely vivid dream of the previous night. He looked at the ash tree. No baby. No straw cradle. He had slept in the exact same spot where the cradle had been.

With the sun shining and birds singing, it was difficult to conjure up the memory of the witch and her outrageous performance of the night before. Slowly Egar stood up, looking at the tree. There it was—the cleft through which the crone had passed the baby.

He stood there trying to make some sense of his dream. The more he remembered of its remarkable details, the more he experienced a strange feeling of *déjà vu*. He had experienced this rite, not last night, but long ago. Egar was more puzzled than ever. How could he have previously witnessed the unusual pagan ritual when he had never before been to Gellert's grave beside the giant ash?

Slowly the meaning dawned. The woman he saw last night was his mother. Many years before when her baby was deathly ill she risked all to find a cure for it. She brought the sick infant to the forest, handing him to the wood witch. His mother understood if the cure worked, she could take home a healthy baby the next morning. If the spirits were not strong enough to protect the baby, wild animals would find and devour it during the night. The risk was small. Without miraculous intervention the baby would not live out the night at any rate. The greater risk was that during the night the wood sprites might steal her baby, leaving in its place a fairy brat, a changeling.

The feeling of illness with which Egar had awakened returned to him in a rush. Now he understood. His mother brought her ill infant to the sacred ash and the next morning, after the witch's ministrations, instead of her own child, she took him, Egar, home with her. Happy in the hope that her child would grow into a healthy son, she was unaware she had taken home, not her own true son but a changeling.

Egar knelt by the tree and retched. Now he understood why his mother had looked at him with such loathing, not wanting him to spend one night more in her home. He realized at last what everyone in his family had known for many years. He was not human but a fairy brat!

Oh, God! How could this be? Egar stumbled to his horse. Only one place offered an answer. He must return to his Old Master. If anyone could make sense of this insane situation, it was he. Blindly Egar let the animal find its own way out of the forest to the road. Once there he kicked it as hard as he could. Startled, Smoke began to gallop. Egar kicked again and again.

The thought racketed back and forth in his brain to the drumming of his horse's hooves. A changeling! A changeling! What had the gods done? He was not a boy. Not a man. Not even human—a fairy brat!

Chapter Thirty-One

By the time Egar reached his Master's cave, the sun was high overhead. Breathless and sweating, he tumbled from the horse's back.

"Master! Master!" His legs trembled. He felt vulnerable, like the young child he had once been. In need of the comfort and counsel of a father. Friend. Advisor.

"*Master! Master!*" echoed his voice from the empty cave.

Where could his Old Master be? Surely he has the sight enough, Egar thought with frustration, to know I am here and in dire need of his help.

At the precise moment Egar entered the cave he heard with a thrill of recognition, the nearly forgotten sound of this special place. As if a bird's wing had brushed against a set of blown-glass bells somewhere far off in the interior of the mountain. The magical sound occured only after an extended absence. Egar always thought the cave was saying how glad it was to have him return.

The table stood where it always had, in the center of the room, a bench on either side. His master's sleeping pallet lay against the wall to the left of the opening, where the earliest rays of morning sun would find and awaken him.

Next to that was the chest from which Egar had chosen the magic paraphernalia he had taken with him when he first left to discover the world and his destiny in it. The sight of the large wooden trunk brought a catch to his throat and he quickly crossed the space to touch the battered old relic. It seemed hard to believe he had ever been so young and eager as that lad. He wondered how he had allowed his destiny to become so muddled.

It was easier then, he thought. Ah, Master, come back soon and help me. I once felt invincible but now I have lost the direction to whatever it was the gods wanted for my life.

Egar resumed his inspection deeper into the cave's interior. Nothing in this even darker place showed that he had once slept here away from the main room, so that his master's nocturnal puttering would not disturb a small boy's slumber. Unconsciously Egar looked up to the high ceiling of his chamber, rewarded with the sight of hundreds of small, brilliant points of light glowing in the darkness. He could no more explain now, than he could as a boy, what caused this spectacular brilliance, far from any source of illumination. The glow had often sent him to sleep with a sense of wonder and expectation.

Further on into the interior of the cave was a final, nearly pitch-black chamber. Egar breathed in the fragrance of all kinds of dried foods and herbs stored in the dark recesses of the mountain. Here the temperature was cool and dry summer and winter. Apples and garlic, lavender and sage, and something musk-like and sweet immediately brought his Master to mind.

Emerging, Egar beheld ordinary cooking utensils lying near the fire where they always had. The Old Master has been gone for several days at least, Egar reasoned, feeling the fire stone's cool surface. I wonder where he is and when he will return. Egar was not alarmed at the Master's absence. He was frequently gone—gathering herbs, treating the sick and injured, going where the gods summoned him.

Egar felt better just being in the security of the familiar cave. Somehow the idea he was a fairy brat, whatever that might mean to him, seemed less frightening. I will go to the stream to catch fish and pick some blackberries for supper, he thought. There is plenty of dried food here but a fresh meal will be nice. If the Old Master does return this afternoon, he will have a pleasant surprise.

As Egar prepared supper, grilling the fish he had caught on sticks over the fire, cleaning and putting the berries on the table, he kept returning to the open doorway, searching the horizon for his master. To his sorrow the path remained empty. At last he sat down to a solitary supper.

Afterwards Egar stared into the fire. He tried to conjure up a vision of his master but saw nothing in the flame and smoke. Remembering his previous failure to succeed in simple magic when he had been filled with confusion, he tried again to collect his thoughts and focus his powers. He stared into the fire until he felt his eyeballs becoming hot and dry, meanwhile trying to convince himself that ultimately he could accomplish what he wanted. Finally the beloved face hovered, barely discernable in the smoke. As the white wisps curled and wavered up the wall, the face became distorted and very faint. Just before it disappeared completely Egar sent his message, begging the Master to return to the cave as quickly as possible.

Sitting, unmoving for many minutes after the face and smoke were gone, Egar remembered the good times he had experienced in this cave. A feeling of contentment stole over him.

* * *

Egar awoke to find the sun well up. Coming out into the warmth of a new summer day, he was startled to see a man and boy, sitting on a boulder, watching him.

"What can I do for you?" Egar asked them.

"Be the Old One in?" the man asked. "We be coming soon as we seen the smoke. Me son be needing his healing."

He turned to the half-grown boy who held out his leg, the shin disfigured with a great open sore. Encrusted in dirt, the wound oozed greyish-green puss.

"He is not here," Egar answered. "But I have learned much of his healing art. Perhaps I can help."

"We would be glad for it," the man said. "Me son, Guy, be hurting bad. It worsens day by day."

Gentle as Egar tried to be, the boy winced with pain and clung tightly to his father's hand as the wound was cleansed.

"This needs powder from special fungi to fight the rot," Egar said at last. "I do not have any with me. They must be gathered fresh while early morning dew is still on them. A poultice of soft mosses would help, too. Nevertheless, we can begin the healing with some garlic."

He carefully peeled away the dry skin from several cloves. The sore was too open and painful to be rubbed with the garlic, so he cut thin slices and laid them on top of the injury, winding a length of white linen fabric around the leg.

"Keep this as clean and dry as possible for today," Egar said. "I will gather what I need at first light tomorrow. Come back and I will re-dress it for you."

"Ye be kind," said the man. "We miss the Old One. That we do."

"How long has he been gone?"

"We be seeing no smoke since the end of last winter."

"That long," mused Egar. "I wonder what could possibly have become of him. I have never known him to be absent for more than a fortnight at most. Ah well, I saw his face in the flame last night so I know he is well."

The days gradually grew longer as young Guy and his father returned again and again to Egar in the cave. Each time they came, they brought gifts of food—rabbits they hunted in the woods, fresh bread baked by Guy's grateful mother, vegetables gathered from the garden. Little by little the sore on the boy's leg healed.

Word of Egar's skill in healing spread among the people so that by mid-summer, several had brought gifts of food to him in appreciation for his help.

Egar ate some of what they brought while it was still fresh but he preserved as much as he could. He hung the meat on hooks above the fire so the smoke drifting up would gradually cure it. He spent hours cutting the fruits and vegetables then spread them in thin layers to dry in the hot summer sun. The activity helped pass the solitary hours and he was relieved to know his Old Master would have food for the long winter to come.

Still the Master did not return.

In the evenings, alone in the cave as twilight faded into night, Egar thought of Pepin. He hoped with all his heart the man fared well in captivity, but try as he might, he could not bring Pepin's image into the fire. In his heart he felt he would know if Pepin had come to harm, but he could not verify Pepin's safety by watching him in the flames.

Just as Egar was beginning to feel safe, one of the local farmers came by, bringing a wedge of cheese in thanks for Egar's help in treating his cow.

"I be at the mill near them homes on t'other side of the forest. They be soldiers there. They be askin' had anyone seen aught of a magician who run off after murdering a nobleman close to the king."

Egar felt his body grow cold and rigid. He worked to keep his voice nonchalant. "And what did you tell them?"

"Oh, I be not talking to them soldiers m'self. Them soldiers be right hard to understand, speakin' high an' mighty Latin an' all."

"But surely, someone was with them to translate what they said so townsfolk could understand," persisted Egar.

"Oh, aye, they be someone like that. But how be I knowin' he be sayin' what the soldiers be tellin' him to?" He gave Egar an understanding smile. "When no one be knowin' aught of King Dagobert's sorcerer, I hear them mutter among theyselves. 'Mayhap the man turn heself to an owl and fly off!'

"They act like they no be willing to return to Dagobert without the murderer."

Egar felt his palms dampen and resisted the urge to wipe them against his tunic.

Chapter Thirty-Two

Late one night, Egar, unaccountably restless, stood outside the cave. The summer air was soft and still, the starry heavens alive and sparkling brilliantly. The constellations wheeling overhead reminded him of Stonehenge.

More than the usual number of falling stars filled the sky, their fiery tails like sparks from a mid-summer's eve bonfire. One blaze of light seemed to fall directly beyond the hill on which he stood.

When Egar at last re-entered the cave he was stunned to see his Old Master sitting in his usual place. Egar heaved a sigh. Feeling childishly relieved, he longed only to let the Master shoulder the burden his life had become.

"But, but Master," he stuttered, "when did you arrive? I never saw you coming up the path. But that was probably because I was watching the sky. Did you ever see... But where have you been?"

His master put up a hand. "You will drown me in the torrent pouring from your mouth—as always you were wont to do," he said, not unkindly.

"Oh, Master, forgive me. It is just that I am glad to see you. It has been so long, I was beginning to worry about you. Where have you been?"

"Gone."

"I know you were gone, but where?" asked Egar.

"Not just gone. *Gone.*"

At Egar's uncomprehending look the Old Master said, "Never mind, boy. Perhaps later I will be able to explain it to you. In the meantime, fetch me a drink of water from the spring and put some logs on the fire. I am chilled."

The old man pulled his cloak more closely about himself and shivered.

Egar was contrite. "I should have asked after your needs immediately. Are you sure you want nothing but water?"

"Water is all," the Master replied, "and some heat."

When Egar handed him the goblet he was shocked to realize how frail the old man had grown. He seemed almost transparent, faintly luminous.

Egar heaped more logs on the fire though the cave seemed overly warm to him. "Are you sure you want nothing to eat?" he asked. "Are you all right? Is there anything I can get?"

"I am fine." The Master shrugged his back and shoulders appreciatively in the heat from the fire. "Now, tell me what was so important that it drove you to summon me back," he demanded, sipping the water.

"Oh, Master," Egar said. "You *did* get my message. What a relief! I need your help desperately. So many things I do not understand have happened lately. I fear I am a changeling, a fairy brat. I always thought I was human. Different from others perhaps, but still human. If I am not, how do I perceive myself? How do I act?

"And then there is Pepin who is being held prisoner. He grows older and there may not be time for him to become the king I saw in the vision. In his heart he blames me for it."

Egar paused for half a heartbeat before continuing. "Though I feel for him, surely it is not *my* fault he took the vision so strongly to heart. I never promised *he* would be the king. He said, and I believe him, that Dagobert will cut out my tongue if I dare go back. Do you really think the gods plan *that* as my fate?" Egar shivered and swallowed the nausea that the thought of his tongue being cut out always brought.

He stopped for a moment, looking pensive, then he brightened. "I do know where Gisela is, though I dare not go to her, even in my thoughts. It is not allowed and..."

Suddenly Egar saw his Old Master's eyes close in weariness. With remorse he realized he had allowed his problems to erupt without regard for his Master's obvious fatigue.

In the ensuing silence his Master opened his eyes and said, "Is that all? Are you quite finished?"

"Yes, Master," whispered Egar, feeling humbled.

"Solving your many dilemmas should keep us well occupied through the fall and into next winter." The Master sighed although his eyes twinkled faintly. "Let us take one thing at a time. Now what is this about a fairy brat?"

Egar related the dream he had while asleep under Odin's tree near Gellert's grave. "The woman was my mother and I the babe she took back. Somehow she knew I was not her true son. That is why she reacted as she did when I tried to help her in her illness. But how do I live if I am not human? What should I do?"

Egar's questions hung in the silent air.

"Tell me," the Master finally asked, "what happens if you cut your finger?"

"Blood flows and I feel pain." Egar was puzzled.

"And if you were to be dumped into the middle of a lake?"

"I would sink to the bottom and drown. I know not how to swim."

"And what do you do if you are hungry?"

"Eat, if there is food."

"And how do you feel if someone you love leaves you?"

"Sad." Egar sighed. "I have felt sadness so often."

"What do you make of this?" the Master asked.

There was a moment of silence while Egar pondered and then comprehension dawned.

With a smile he said, "These are all *human* traits! Oh, Master, thank you. Thank you!"

They sat in companionable silence while Egar absorbed the implications. "But why did my mother react to me as she did?"

"See it as she would have. In her ignorance, she took a deathly ill baby to Odin's tree, fearing the forest sprites might exchange it for one of theirs. And when as you grew older, you seemed to have little in common with the rest of the family, her suspicions were confirmed."

"Is that why she did not call me back when I first left to come to you?" Egar asked.

"Yes."

"But why am I so different?"

"Every person is different from every other," said the Master. "Think on it. Of all of the people you have met in your journeys, are any two exactly alike?"

"No, but that does not explain why I seem to have not the slightest thing in common with my parents, or my brother and sister."

"Ah, that is because the gods have selected you to fulfill a unique position," answered the Master. "Because of that they have gifted you with unusual talents."

Egar felt lost, confused. "How do I learn who I am? What I should do?"

The Master smiled. "Pause. Listen to the voices that direct your life. You may find you are doing what the gods have wanted all along."

Egar pondered this in silence. Then he heard once again, in his mind's eye, his Master's parting words.

'Your life will change the course of Frankish history.' He wanted desperately to know what those words signified.

"Master..." he began.

"Yes?"

The words would not come. What if they meant nothing? Egar would appear foolish, giving them weight when they bore none.

"Nothing," he said.

"Then that is enough for one night. Go. Sleep now. The sun will soon be up calling you to your duties."

"Yes, Master."

"I will not be here when you awake. We must all follow the voices that guide us. However, I will return and we will work together to unravel that which you have tangled."

"Oh, Master, I am so grateful you heard my call and came back to help me. I am truly sorry if I interrupted your work but what I saw was so disturbing it made me feel more than ill. You were the only one I could turn to for help."

Egar spent what was left of the night in untroubled, dreamless sleep. For the first time in many months he felt whole and at peace with himself.

What shall I do today? Egar pondered as he emerged into the empty front chamber of the cave. He gazed at the bench on which his master had sat the previous evening. It stood where he left it next to the fire, now cold.

That is what I shall do. I will gather wood to store for his fire this coming winter. His bones are old and vulnerable to the cold. He will require a large stack to keep them warm.

I wonder where *I* shall be when winter comes? Unable to answer that question, he decided to concentrate on making what he could of today and leave the future in the hands of the gods.

Searching the nearby forest, he found a fallen oak. As Egar chopped with his hand ax, he was soon covered with a glistening sheen of sweat. The exercise made him feel alive and glowing with energy. By late afternoon he had a bundle of thick branches loaded on the horse's back.

The setting sun cast long shadows far ahead as, heavily laden, he slowly climbed the path to the cave. He was rewarded by heavenly scents rising from a bubbling pot. The Master had the table laid for supper.

"If you are ever in need of a new position," Egar exclaimed cheerfully, "you could always find employment in the kitchen at court. You know secrets of herbs and seasonings worthy of a king's banquet."

"I shall keep the recommendation in mind, in case I find myself in such a situation," his master remarked dryly. "Come eat. You look in need of nourishment."

They sat in comfortable silence after their meal.

"Now what did I hear of a vision, a great king, and some man named Pepin?" the Master asked.

Egar described how he had come to be in Clothar's court and what he had seen on that fateful night.

"Do you think the king of my vision is the legend to come which the priest of Stonehenge mentioned?" asked Egar.

"What did the priest say?"

"'Britain's legend has come and gone but it will live on in poetry and song. Frankish Gaul's legend has yet to be, but once come, in history's chronicles will it known forever be.'"

"If the gods will it, your vision could well be that legend," the Master said. He looked thoughtfully across the room. A smile seemed to tug at his lips.

"But legends are about ancient gods or saints, and of lives lived long ago," Egar protested.

"True," agreed the Master. "But have you thought that you and I will be long-dead ancients to those who live far in the future?"

Egar pondered his Master's words. "It is hard to think of such a time," he whispered.

"But how did, what is his name, Pepin, come to know of your vision?"

"I told him," Egar replied.

"You told him? But why?"

"He asked."

"Do you always tell your innermost thoughts to anyone who asks?" His Master's voice carried a tone of amazement.

"Pepin is older than I and in a position of authority. Besides, it had to do with him. He had a right to know."

"Hmmm," meditated the Master, his chin resting on a wrinkled old hand. "*I* would have waited telling anyone until I knew more about what the sight signified."

Egar felt concern as he began to understand that by his actions he bore responsibility for what had eventually befallen Pepin.

"But then," continued the Master, "if the gods had wanted caution they would have sent someone with the wisdom that comes with age and experience rather than an impetuous, half-grown youth."

"Then you think I might not have ruined the plans of the gods by telling Pepin?"

"It would take more than that to ruin their plans, my boy. No, I suspect for some reason known only to themselves, they wanted this Pepin of yours to do just as he did, make of his office a position of power and substance."

Egar sighed with relief.

The ancient one continued, "Why the gods would then allow him to be imprisoned for his trouble, I have no idea. They have a strange sense of humor and it probably amuses them to see us mortals fumbling about down here."

Egar smiled at the thought.

"You might not have done as badly as you think. Though it would not be amiss if you would pause and ponder before you leap."

Egar bowed his head in acknowledgement of this, his greatest fault.

"What will be my part in the great king's reign?"

"That I cannot tell you," the Master replied. "Look into your heart. It will know."

The silence was broken only by the crackling of dancing flames.

"It tells me nothing," Egar finally admitted.

"It will, when it is ready. And then you will know your destiny," the Master reassured him.

Egar felt a thrill of anticipation, wondering when it would happen. Silence fell once again comfortably between them.

"You no longer need me," said the Master at last. "I was already free of earth's bonds, within sight of great light and fully aware of the warm welcome awaiting me when you called me back."

Understanding dawned on Egar.

"Do you mean that you were... you are...," he began, then, "No! You cannot die. I *need* you. Without you I am muddled and confused."

Egar put out his arms as if to physically restrain his beloved Master from passing out of his world.

The Master held up a translucent hand to stop him. "Do not try to hold me back," he said. "It is time and I am eager for it. I have done as the gods directed and it is good. You are more a man than you realize. I long for the warmth and the light which beckons me. Let me go with your blessing." He gazed fondly into brown eyes, brimming with unshed tears.

With an effort Egar blinked them back, tasting salt running down his throat. "*Mia culpa*," he whispered. "I was selfish. You, if anyone, have earned the right to go wherever it is that calls you. I will not stop you nor wish you back."

As Egar said this the beloved form of his master became transparent and elongated until it blended into the smoke of the fire. For a moment only, it trembled there and then was gone.

Egar stood, facing the spot where the Master had been, tears falling unheeded down his cheeks. Tears, not so much of grief as gratitude. He realized he had been blessed by the gods at having been allowed to share in his master's life. He sent a message of love out into the great unknown and, as if in benediction, felt his own body empty itself of sorrow and become buoyant with bittersweet joy.

Chapter Thirty-Three

As leaves turned from bright gold to lifeless brown, Egar set about making his cave ready for the wind and snow to come. He spread a thick cushion of cut threshings on the floor and made a new threshold from a split log to keep both the flooring in and the damp cold out. Leather curtains were lashed to pegs driven in around the cave openings.

Egar felt like a rabbit in its burrow as he surveyed his cozy nest. The thick-walled cave, so well insulated from drafts and damp, would keep him warm enough with only the heat of the cooking fire.

However, he had no stable for his horse. During the summer Smoke was content enough tethered out-of-doors, but soon she would need shelter from the frigid blasts of winter. At last, Egar led his horse to Guy's family to board there in exchange for free use of her come plowing time next spring.

As autumn rains turned into the snow of winter, Egar felt proud of how well he was able to cope. But when daylight hours grew ever shorter and silent snows became howling blizzards, the solitary hours spent in the womb of his cave began to pall.

To pass the time he practiced magic tricks neglected since leaving Metz. He was shocked at how slowly his fingers moved. The self-imposed discipline gave him a sense of purpose and made the time go faster. But once he regained his dexterity, further practice seemed pointless without an audience.

If only he had a companion. At the palace in Paris there were too many people, too much noise and confusion. Here the solitude and silence were equally tiresome. Egar fancied his long ago arrival might have been a welcome diversion for the Master. Not that his childish company had in any way been equal to the gifts of learning with which the old man had showered him. It made him glad to think he had, without being aware of it, perhaps made the years spent together more pleasant for the Wise One.

Egar needed something to dispel his restiveness. Then he knew. His fingers ached for the touch of harp strings and an idea was born. He would make one!

Pulling his hat down around his ears and his well-worn travel cloak closer about his shoulders, Egar braved the cold outside to brush away the mounds of snow from the pile of logs, searching for the stout oak which he had yet to cut into lengths for the fire.

He worked up a healthy sweat chopping it into three roughly equal parts for the triangular shape he needed.

That night as he ate his supper he looked again and again at the rough logs. He thought out each step he would take to create from them an instrument fit for a king's court, whether or not he was destined ever to play it there. As he fell asleep he dreamed of the smooth perfection of the finished harp, felt the strings vibrating under his fingers and heard heavenly music, a lullaby from the gods.

Now he arose each morning, keen to set to work on the harp. Time fairly flew and come evening, Egar would be surprised to find himself working in a nearly dark cave as the torches sputtered, the cooking fire reduced to mere glowing embers. Painstakingly he hollowed out the sounding board, smoothed the wood, fashioned the tuning pegs.

On days when a weak sun cast oblique shadows across the snow-covered landscape, Egar set traps for rabbits. Much as he enjoyed the freshly roasted meat and could use the skins for blankets, more important were the intestines which would become his harp's strings. Cutting, twisting, stretching and drying the gut took days.

Finally, it was ready. One by one, he tuned the strings. Filled with elation Egar plucked chord after chord from the instrument, born of his hands. The harp seemed to have a soul of its own, satisfying the hunger that solitude had caused to fester inside him. Egar smiled, no longer alone.

Gradually winter snows changed to spring rain, frozen ground turned to mud and the world smelled new again. The neighboring farmers returned to the cave and were pleased at how well the Young Master had endured the isolation of winter.

When he walked across the valley to retrieve Smoke, Guy's mother commented on his hair, grown long and shaggy from a whole winter of neglect. "Sweet cherubim! I never seen a man with such long hair in all me days!"

Embarrassed, Egar ran his fingers through his hair. He was shocked to find it had grown past his shoulders and half-way down his back. "With long hair the king's privilege, it would go ill with me to have one of Dagobert's guards see me like this!"

"I can cut it," the farmer's wife offered.

"Please. I would be forever in your debt."

"And the brown beard? Shaved clean? Cut short? Or left long? She stood, hands on hips, studying him through squinted eyes. "Long be makin' ye look like a young Master. That it do."

"Trimmed short, I think. There is plenty of time yet for me to resemble the Old One."

* * *

With paths once more passable the valley folk flocked to him for ground willow bark to ease the pain and fever of grippe or shepherd's purse to staunch the flux accompanying illnesses that lasted well into spring.

As the years passed, though he came to terms with his lonely life, Egar longed for a companion, a mate. There were times when his loins ached with desire and his heart hammered in his chest. If asked, he would have said it happened most often in the dead and dark of winter but then, also in the spring when every living thing seemed to have a mate and new things were born to frolic all around him. He felt it, too, during the warm evenings of summer when he thought longingly of having someone soft and gentle to hold.

One summer evening Egar was riding home when he sniffed the aroma of cooking food. Rounding a bend, he was perplexed. The delicious smelling smoke was coming from within his own cave!

Who would dare enter his domain? Surely not the nearby peasants. They always waited respectfully outside. They would have dreaded the consequences of the magic within. So it must be someone from far away who had no fear of him. Pepin? A messenger from the king? Someone sent by the gods?

His mind in a swirl of anticipation, Egar stopped just inside the doorway, blinking in the sudden gloom. His jaw dropped as he saw, not Pepin, not a messenger in the uniform of any court, not even the bearded visage of a wise one. Instead he gaped at a young woman, equally startled, still bent over the bubbling cooking pot.

Egar had a muddled impression of wide hazel eyes, smooth cheeks flushed crimson with the heat of the fire, tendrils of brown curls framing a face moist with perspiration. In a moment the surprised look gave way to one of pleasure as the young woman straightened and smiled, producing a dimple. She seemed to be expecting him.

"Who... what..." Egar sputtered.

Her smile gave way to an infectious laugh. "Welcome home."

"Who are you and why are you here?"

Her laughter pealed once more. "The gods sent me, in answer to your request."

"My request? What request? I never..."

"Well, your longing for a mate must be ever so strong then."

"Oh, it is," agreed Egar with his whole heart. "But I would never have presumed to *ask* for a maiden. I assumed the gods meant me to live a celibate life."

"There are gods who expect that of their followers. But not ours," she explained.

"Do you mean I could have anything I wanted just by longing for it?" Egar asked, amazed.

Once more the dimple appeared. "Oh, no. But every now and again the gods want for us what we long for ourselves and when that happens—she paused as though searching for just the right word, "—miracles occur."

"What is *this* miracle's name?"

"Dione." Before he could think of anything else to say, she invited, "Come. Eat."

They speared pieces of meat and vegetables with their knives and sopped up the juice with chunks of bread.

"How came you here?" Egar asked finally. "Where did you come from?"

Dione's face stilled, her eyes staring thoughtfully into the distance. "In my fifteenth year my father gave me to an old man whose wife died in childbirth, her infant with her. The man was a kind husband to me in his way."

She paused. "We lived together for some time but the gods granted us no children. Finally, one winter, he sickened. I bathed his fever with cool water and gave him warm tea and honey to drink. I tried to stop his cough with a poultice of mustard and garlic but it was not enough, and he had not the will to live."

She looked sad. Egar imagined her struggle to save the life of a dispirited old man.

"I returned home to my family, overcome with sorrow. Had I tried harder, known more, perchance I might have saved my husband's life." Dione looked lost and pensive. "My family was less than overjoyed to see me."

Egar thought of his own family's reaction to his return and knew instinctively the pain her simple phrase conveyed. He reached out and took her hand in his.

Dione smiled. "They were not at fault. The land they till is rocky and yields little food. In the end they could not feed all of us and they must needs keep my brother and his wife. He is the stronger and brings in animals from hunting and does most of the farming. And so I left, alone. The gods led me here."

"Were you not afraid to enter a magician's cave?" Egar asked.

"Of what should I be afraid? You save life. You would never harm it."

Egar felt a warmth in his chest as if his heart, once frozen, had begun to thaw.

When the cave darkened, Dione disrobed in preparation for sleep. Egar watched. Awed.

To his mortification, the sight of Dione's soft, naked body with its full breasts and plump hips caused his male part to became stiff and engorged creating an unmistakable bulge under his tunic. Embarrassment stained his cheeks crimson and he turned away, trying to hide his predicament from her.

Smiling gently, Dione turned him to face her and said, "It must have been a long time since you laid with a woman."

Egar sighed. "A *very* long time."

Dione's gentle laugh sounded as if the wind had brushed a chord from the harp sitting in the corner.

"Come now, off with these clothes. You have naught of which to be ashamed."

Egar did as she directed. He hesitated to touch her until she took his hand and led him to the palet on the floor.

"You *are* a gift of the gods!" Egar allowed his hands to carress her face. Her breasts. The triangle of her womanhood.

In response, Dione kissed him tenderly, pressing her body close to his.

As he entered her, Egar felt an explosion of pleasure. The lips to her opening were firm yet soft and warm as they massaged his extended man-organ. His pungent fluid shot forth unbidden as if, like his heart, it was brought back to life by the magic act of penetrating Dione's hidden place.

Egar shuddered and pushed deeper, allowing all his feelings of loneliness and longing to be ejaculated from the depths of their hiding places within his body. He came again and again, draining years of need before he finally pulled himself free of her.

Filled with an unfamiliar sense of peace, Egar gathered Dione's warm body into the curve of his own. Her head lay on his chest, his arm protectively around her waist, fingers exploring the triangle of curly hair surrounding the wonderful opening.

Tension that he had not realized he was carrying slipped away from him as if he had been allowed to put down an immensely heavy burden. He drifted into a gentle slumber. No dream, no matter how extraordinary, could possibly compete with the reality that lay within his arms.

Chapter Thirty-Four

By the time Egar awoke the next morning, the summer sun shone full on the cave floor and his rumpled pallet. For a few moments he was confused, trying to figure out why he had slept so late, why he felt so unaccountably content. Then it rushed back to him—the maiden, Dione, who had ministered to his unbearable need, who had made his life complete.

He awoke fully. Today would be like no other day had ever been, and tomorrow and all the tomorrows following. He was no longer alone. The gods were kind and good. They had sent him someone to love, someone with whom to share his thoughts, his life—Dione.

Eagerly he looked about the cave. Except for the sunlight it was empty of any life but his own. Dione's clothes, carelessly tossed aside the previous night were gone, as was she. For a moment Egar wondered if she really *had* been there, or was she a fantasy of his deep longing?

But no, she had been real and warmly solid. Egar experienced a gut-wrenching loss. Surely the gods would not allow him but one night of ecstasy. He felt deprived, cheated. He would rather not have been given a gift the loss of which left him feeling so bereft.

Disconsolately, Egar went to the spring to wash his face. He sat on a boulder, reliving every moment from the time he had first seen Dione. No! Even if it *were* only for one night, he could not wish she had never come. He would be thankful for the wondrous gift and not begrudge the night solely because he could have her no longer.

A distant figure on the trail below caught his eye. Dione was coming back!

He raced to her. "I was afraid you had gone away. I thought I might never see you again. I was desolate!"

"Fret not," she replied, smiling. "When I leave, never to return, you will know. I am wont to come and go. There are many wonderful places to explore. Just see what I found this morning!"

Dione held up a basket of blackberries, ripe and shining. "And I was able to pick enough to trade some with a farmer's wife for this—" she held up a jug of thick, fresh cream, "—to go with the berries. We shall break our fast with a meal fit for the gods."

Egar became used to her enthusiasm. When traveling about the hills and valley he looked solely for plants with healing properties, but when they went together she helped him notice his surroundings in a new way. She made things with no value other than their beauty, the focus of his attention. She seemed filled with a compelling *joie de vivre.* While Egar sang to entertain, to earn his supper, Dione sang while doing household activities as if her happiness could not be contained. Her melodies spilled in a warm contralto that seemed to Egar like drops of honey.

Dione returned one day from exploring the countryside. "Oh, Egar," she cried, "the gods have shown me the most perfect place! You must see it."

He pulled her close to him. Her soft breasts pressed against his chest as she returned his embrace and, standing on tiptoes, kissed his mouth.

Each time she went off on her own Egar felt a twinge of anxiety, terrified that one time she might not come back. She would only laugh and admonish him not to fear. Had she not promised he would know when they were to part? In the meantime he lived in a perpetual state of dread. He strove valiantly not to allow her into his heart, fearing the pain when she chose to disappear. But how could he not? He realized it was already too late.

"What is this wonderful place that I must see?" he queried.

"I cannot describe it. You must see it for yourself. Can we go tomorrow? Early in the morning?"

Egar, ever practical, thought they should be taking advantage of the good weather to prepare food for the winter. Then, with a pang he wondered if she would still be there to share the cave when winter came. Picturing himself alone again made him shudder. Taking a deep breath he determined to concentrate on the day at hand rather than on his fears of what the future might hold.

"Of course. Tomorrow," he agreed.

Leaving the trail, they skirted low-growing branches, before finally arriving at the spot she had discovered deep within the forest.

They stood silently side by side for several moments, absorbing the beauty of the enchanted place. The sun sparkled on a small waterfall cascading into a clear pool. Flowers bloomed among the ferns on the moss-covered banks. In dappled shade an open space welcomed the robe they spread upon the ground.

Egar spoke in a hushed voice. "However did you find this spot?"

"The gods led me here," she replied simply.

Quickly they stripped off their clothing and entered the sun-warmed water of the crystal pool. They laughed as they splashed each other like small children.

Once returned to the bank, lying on their robe, Egar could bear it no longer. "Dione, please say you will stay with me always. I love you too much to let you go. I would be married to you, promising 'till death do us part' if you would but love me."

"Of course I love you," she responded.

Joy flooded Egar. He opened his arms and she fitted into them as if they had been created only to hold her. Egar bent down to kiss her lips. Hers welcomed him.

"We are as much mates as those who are wed by a priest of the One God," she said. "Our gods have brought us together."

"Are we to be so 'until death do us part'?" asked Egar.

"Who can read the future?" asked Dione. "We must but live our destiny. The gods will grant us what time they will."

Egar felt parting at any time would be far too soon. Then desire overcame his concern. He could not be gloomy in the face of her obvious love for him.

"Then I will treasure our love—for as long as the gods grant." He finally admitted they, not he, controlled the length of their life together.

They kissed and tenderly consummated their sylvan marriage.

Chapter Thirty-Five

As Egar and Dione made their way back to their cave, they invited the valley families to come share in their celebration.

Once home, Egar built a huge fire outside. By the time their neighbors brought their gifts of food, the coals would be glowing and evenly hot.

Families arrived from near and far. Trestle tables set up under the trees were soon laden with sliced fresh onions and vegetables pickled in brine. Pies stuffed with roasted partridges, quail, skylarks and thrushes took places of honor. Had it been a grand feast at court, the birds might have been put in alive, to fly out when the pie was cut open.

Dessert pies filled with peaches and berries crowded one end of a table while at the other, bread was stacked like cord wood.

Smoke from roasting meat stuffed with nuts and raisins sparked appetites. The bota of verjuice passed from hand to hand and someone tapped a cask of ale. Voices grew louder, the laughter more frequent.

Perhaps it was the smell of meat cooking or the unusual crowd of people, but suddenly, in his mind's eye, Egar recalled scenes from his life at court.

Looking about he thought to himself, nowhere I have ever lived has the food tasted better, the air smelled sweeter, were the people kinder than right here on this hillside. Not for one minute do I miss life in the great halls of royalty.

When everyone had finished eating, Egar brought out his harp. Dione carried her wooden flute while Gundobad's son retrieved his drum from the ox-cart. The three of them began a slow syncopated tune. Bodies swayed to the rhythm as hands clapped softly. Several women began dancing to the sinuous melody. Gradually the tempo grew faster as Egar led the way into a lively jig. The drum picked up the beat and Dione followed, weaving her melody in and out. Everyone joined in the dance. On and on they circled and stomped until all were panting and out of breath.

"Three cheers for the musicians!"

The crowd roared their approval.

"Someone pass the ale before I die of thirst," a voice cried out above the good-natured banter.

Tankards of verjuice and leather botas of wine passed from hand to hand.

"A song," someone begged.

"Yes! A song."

"Well, then," Egar said, "a song it is, if my lovely Dione will join me in it."

They sang well together, Dione's alto to Egar's baritone. The harp wove chords that bound their voices into one. Ballads of lost love and lullabies soon soothed babes to sleep, cradled in their mother's laps.

The party broke into groups. Older children ran races in the meadow while women rested in the shade. Egar joined the men gathered around wagons in deep discussion.

"I say King Dagobert be deranged," argued Gundobad.

"Aye," agreed another. "He be sending his soldiers at all times of the year to collect tribute."

"And not to pay for armies to march and conquer new lands for the crown, *I* be hearing," said Guy. "But for decorating churches and buying jewels for his mistresses!"

"And worse, too, if rumor be true!"

Unbidden, a rush of memories flooded through Egar—Dagobert as a small child laughing delightedly, throwing balls for Egar to juggle before Clothar and the court; the young prince dressed in wedding white escorting Gomatrud, his betrothed, into Metz; the corpulent king who held the threat of life or death over both Pepin and himself.

"If it be not for the good Queen Nanthild, we Franks be in a sorry state, me thinks."

"She be making most decisions for poor, sorry Dagobert. That be what I heard."

Egar saw the redheaded woman in his mind's eye, flirting with the corpulent king at the long-ago banquet. So the lovely Nanthild—from chambermaid, to maiden of the chamber, to queen—has done far better than anyone would have given her credit for.

"Where do you hear such tales?" he asked.

"At the mill," replied Gundobad.

"And from others who live nearer the main road," added another.

"In all this, have you heard aught of a nobleman from Austrasia who goes by the name of Pepin the Vain?" queried Egar.

"Aye. He be mayor of the palace of Austrasia, brought to Metz by the nobles there against the will of crazy King Dagobert," responded Gundobad. "Knew ye him when ye be part of Dagobert's court?"

Egar felt a swirl of confusion. "But how guessed you I came from there?"

"Ye be recalling when first ye came I heard soldiers at the mill asking aught about a murdering sorcerer, missing from the king's service? Well, that be ye, be it not?"

"But I thought you did not understand their court Latin," said Egar.

"Understanding of them from the king comes and goes, me be thinking." Gundobad smiled, a knowing look in his eyes.

Guy's father added, "Back then, they be saying the sorcerer be riding a splotchy grey horse. That be yer Smoke, be it not?"

"Yer healing and the magic, they be not common neither," added Guy, not to be outdone.

"Do you mean you have suspected all along that I was the sorcerer for whose capture the king offered ransom?"

Heads nodded.

"But why did you not tell those soldiers when first they asked about me?"

A look of shock came to every face.

"We be not betraying one of our own!" exclaimed Gundobad.

Egar was amazed. "But the treasure offered was more than you could make in a lifetime!"

"Ye be healing me leg when first ye came," said Guy as if that explained everything.

"If ye *be* a sorcerer, ye be it for the good of the likes o' we. Whatever the king's claim, ye did no deserve to be led back in chains," added his father.

"So Pepin is once more mayor of the palace," mused Egar, more to himself than the others.

"Aye," affirmed several voices.

"But if not for King Dagobert, who rules?" he asked.

"Dagobert rules Neustria and Burgundy, and be having claim o'er all we Franks," explained one man.

"But his son, Sigibert, be king there," finished Guy's father.

Egar thought of Gomatrud, sent to a convent and her three-year-old child crowned king of Austrasia. "How old is he now?"

"Mayhap nine or ten."

Egar had a sudden, piercing memory of his vision of the great king. He winced in pain from the strength of the sight, his eyes momentarily blinded. "I must return to Metz. To Pepin. He is more in need of me now than ever he was before!"

"But ye cannot!" cried Gundobad. "To go to court, any court, would let Dagobert know where ye be. The king be dangerous and vindictive. He fear *ye* more than he do Pepin."

"Aye," interrupted Guy. "I hear he claims you be putting a curse on him. Dagobert blames all misery what befalls him on that sorcerer who murdered his closest advisor, then ran away from his great hall in Paris."

"Better ye be staying here in our valley," added Guy's father, "with us who would keep ye safe."

Egar was torn. The cave and these good people promised refuge. But he knew he must allow his destiny to play itself out.

It is your destiny after all. Only you can decide to what extent you will allow it to be your guide, said his master's voice within Egar's head.

"Mayhap ye be too good for the likes of we," said Guy's father quietly.

"Aye. If it be yer life to go, we be not holding ye," agreed Gundobad sadly. "Ye may have sommat of importance to be doing where kings and such be living."

"Your life will change the course of Frankish history." The master's voice rang with conviction.

"Although the forces for evil are strong, you can influence that which works for good in history if you fail not the challenge of your destiny," echoed the voice of the priest of Stonehenge.

But what of Dione? argued a part of him. There will be danger there for her also. Was this one short summer together all the gods had in mind?

"I *must* go to Pepin," Egar said with a heavy heart. "I still have no understanding of my destiny, but it is as tied to Pepin now as it ever was. Of that I am certain."

He looked beyond the men to all who had gathered for his wedding feast. "Though I go from here, know—each of you—that your gifts of trust and friendship mean more to me than anything I could have offered you and yours."

That evening as Dione and Egar sat alone in front of the flickering fire he told her of his need to return to Pepin in Metz.

"I cannot deny the danger," he said. "Dagobert is perilously demented. And he views *me* with especial hatred." Egar gagged, light-headed at the remembered smell of blood and excrement. Gelasius, dead at his feet. His own knife plunged into the nobleman's gut. "I cannot ask you to come."

Egar felt a withering as part of him slowly died. He waited for her response, unable to breathe.

Dione did not move, but sat staring into the glowing coals as if seeking an answer from the gods. Finally she stirred. "I will go with you. I have never been so far as Metz. It sounds an interesting escapade."

Hope surged in Egar's miraculously healed heart. "Dione, my love, my own. I am overjoyed!" He pulled away, looking deep into her eyes. "But I would not have you at risk."

"I look *foreward* to such an adventure. Especially since I shall share it with you." She looked at him fondly. "The gods will lead us. And if the way be chancy," she shrugged, "that, too, must be their plan."

Chapter Thirty-Six

When Egar and Dione arrived in Metz they found the courtyard of the royal compound frantically busy. It looked to Egar like a disturbed anthill.

"What is the cause of this pandemonium?" he asked a passing guard.

"The kingdom be in chaos." The guard paused. "King Dagobert in Paris be incapacitated and confined to chambers. They be sending for his confessor priest."

I should be sad, Egar thought, but all I feel is relief.

Clearly exasperated, the guard said, "It be too much! First Pepin. Then Dagobert. It be"—he threw up his hands as if asking God's help "—hopeless!"

"What is?" asked a perplexed Egar. "Why 'hopeless'?"

"Be ye deaf, dumb and blind, man?" asked the guard. "Our Pepin, too. The whole kingdom knows. Pepin be dying!"

Stunned, Egar had no time to digest this alarming news before the once lovely Itta rushed out. At first he scarcely recognized her. In the years since he had last seen her she had aged perceptibly. Her cheeks were gaunt and creases bracketed her mouth. Her hair was no longer dark but grey.

When she saw him, a smile of relief changed her into a semblance of her former self. "Egar! Thank Sweet Mary and all her saints! You came in time. Pepin asks for you and we knew not where to find you—nor even if you were yet alive."

Without inquiring into his life since she had last seen him, Itta immediately led him across the great hall to the steps leading to the gallery above.

Egar glanced back to see the major domo directing Dione to a bench to wait.

Pepin's chamber was cast in shadows. A knot of men, a priest, a guard, and one whom Egar took to be a physician, stood talking quietly in one corner. The great bed dominated the small room. A page hovered nearby.

"Egar has arrived," Itta announced as they entered. "I feel sure Pepin will want to be alone with him."

She brushed aside the protests of the three men. "He has been given extreme unction, been bled so often it is a wonder he has any life fluid left, and he can be guarded from without the chamber. You have nothing to fear from Egar. So out, out, all of you!"

Taking the page by the hand she followed the disgruntled group.

Egar went to the side of the bed and gazed at his old friend and mentor. The hair, once a vital red-blond, lay lank and gray upon the pillow. His beard grew sparse on sunken cheeks. Dark smudges underlined his closed eyes. He moaned and winced in pain.

Egar opened the worn travel bag hanging across his shoulder. He found the packet he sought and carefully measured some of its contents into the goblet on the table nearby.

Gently, he lifted Pepin's head and offered a draught of the soothing mixture.

"At least I can see to it you suffer no pain."

Pepin's eyes fluttered open. Their clear brilliance had faded to a cloudy blue. Recognizing Egar, he said in a weak voice, "I failed. I... I never gained the crown."

"Speak not of failure." Egar swallowed the lump filling his throat. "There was a time when I was sure it was *I* who had failed. But my Old Master came back from beyond the edges of this world to help me see that we, all of us, live the parts assigned us in the gods' grand design. Be in peace about that. However, I think it is time we tell your family about the prophecy."

"But you cannot," cried Pepin, rousing himself. "It... must remain secret."

"Secret from the world, but not from those for whom it may yet have meaning."

"You have more to tell? You... have seen the future?"

"Not seen it, at least not as clearly as once I did the vision. But enough to surmise that what I once foretold is far from over."

"Then," agreed Pepin, "call them. But take care what you say!"

Itta arrived first. Tears streaked her cheeks. She rushed to embrace her husband while he yet had strength to recognize her.

Pepin's daughter Bega entered, a twenty-year-old matron. Her son, Young Pepin, clung to her hand. Ansegisel followed. The moppet began to climb up on the bed putting his plump arms around his grandfather.

"No, Pepin," cried Bega, trying to disentangle him.

Egar thought back to the very first day he had met Pepin and his family. Grimwald had been a baby just Young Pepin's age on that day when he had foreseen Bega's conception. Now, except for her startling blue eyes, she looked as her mother had when told that she was with child.

Grimwald and his wife arrived breathless and distraught.

Egar stood silent, thinking of Pepin's family. Would Young Pepin be the king of his vision? One could do worse than choose a grandchild of Old Pepin and Arnulf, once Bishop of Metz, as the greatest king of all time.

Itta sat holding her husband's hand, looking into his eyes with concern. Egar brought a stool for Bega who gratefully sank onto it. Grimwald paced about the chamber, hands behind his back. His nervous energy made him more than ever like Pepin.

When everyone was settled, Egar told them about the long-ago prophecy. "I naturally assumed the vision meant Pepin would be king. My Old Master would have said that, in my youth, I impetuously jumped to that conclusion," he added with a wry smile.

"But if, as it turned out, my father was not to be king, then what was the meaning of it?" queried Grimwald.

"Someone of Pepin's seed will fulfill the prophecy. Perhaps his son—" Egar gave Grimwald a questioning look, "—or a grandson."

Bega's head came up with a small jerk.

"If the prophecy is to be fulfilled, whether we will it or not—," asked Itta, "—why are you telling us? Should we not wait for events to evolve?"

"It must remain a secret," acknowledged Egar. "But you must know of it. Pepin thought himself a failure because he did not become king.

"Far from failing," continued Egar, "Pepin succeeded beyond anyone's expectations. People will read of Pepin in Francia's history. One day they will marvel that he alone wrestled the power to rule from the Merovingian throne and firmly established it in the office of Mayor of the Palace."

There was a moment of reflective silence. Pepin looked as if a heavy burden had been lifted from his tired shoulders.

"With Grimwald to inherit the post," said Egar, "people clearly expect it to remain within the family.

What better position from which to give birth to the future king?"

"But," said Itta, "you still have not answered the question. Why tell you us this now?"

"Not to tempt you to risk all and seize the crown before it is ordained," warned Egar. "But with foreknowledge you may gain further power the future king might need to become the greatest in Frankish history."

Once again the room was plunged into silence. Egar understood his message was formidable. The world they had known was suddenly a different place.

"Where will you be?" asked Itta. "You have given us a glimpse of the future. What is your place in it?"

Egar gave her a startled glance. She appeared composed. Perhaps because the future was out of her hands she could look at it so objectively.

"I have wondered that for many years. Long ago, before I came to Paris and Clothar's court, a priest of Stonehenge sent me forth with a prophecy of his own for my life. I did not understand. But now the meaning of the prophecy is clear.

Britain's legend has come and gone but it will live on in poetry and song. Frankish Gaul's legend has yet to be, but once come, in history's chronicles will it known forever be.

Egar's eyes were met by puzzled glances. "Britain's legendary Arthur is already so obscured by word of mouth, the real man is beyond recalling. But the king of my vision will be our realm's legend. Not remembered in songs only, his life will be writ in ink on parchment. My destiny is to witness that every word is put to parchment. Through the ages, even to the twilight of the world, people will know the truth of our great king."

"But then," said Bega, "it must happen in your lifetime."

"Yes." Egar was acutely aware he looked little older than he had on the day when he saw the seed that would become Bega growing in Itta's womb. "And the story, for all to read, will begin with Pepin. Everyone will marvel at how, all unknowing, he took such steps to prepare for the king who would follow him."

"When they read of your prophecy, they will understand why I worked to acquire the power to rule," said Pepin.

"They will not read of the prophecy," replied Egar. "The monks who write the chronicles will be told only of your actions, not of the prophecy or my part in it.

"Word of that must never escape beyond those in direct blood-line of Pepin's loins. If they were to hear, the Merovingians and their supporters would try to kill you all. And me as well, for the part I played. We must take an oath binding us to secrecy."

"Now?" asked Grimwald.

"No, tonight, at the darkest hour, just after Matins. I will make the necessary preparations. Take heed that none be wakened as you make your way here to Pepin's room."

"But what of us?" asked Ansegisel, indicating himself and Grimwald's wife. We are not of Pepin's line."

"True. But you have children who are. Should your spouse predecease you, it may well fall to you to guide them to their destiny. It behooves you to know of it, and thus be trusted with the secret."

Gravely, each went to Pepin before leaving. His face was pain-free. And although the gossamer wings of death still shrouded him, his visage was of peaceful acceptance of the inevitable. Itta and Bega stooped to kiss him gently. Grimwald took his hand in a grip the intensity of which told all.

Sigibert's court took some time to settle themselves that night. At last everyone slept, rolled in blankets on the floor of the great hall or on pallets in alcoves and huts within the palisades. In Pepin's chamber preparations for the oath were complete.

Egar wore his old magical robe of black and silver. Seven candles burned in a glowing circle in the center of the table. The only other objects on it were a chalice of burnished metal, a knife with a spider motif, the sharp blade reflecting back the fire of the candlelight, and a saucer.

Silently, five figures glided into the room. Allowing their hooded capes to fall to the floor, Bega and Itta were revealed in simple white gowns while Grimwald had worn an overtunic of deep blood red. Without a word they gathered on each side of Pepin's bed, Ansegisel and Grimwald's wife unobtrusively at the outer edges of the family circle.

"We are gathered," Egar intoned, "to willingly take an oath of secrecy. If any word of what we know of the future escapes our lips, the family of Pepin will surely be wiped from the face of the earth."

Egar paused, allowing each of them to understand fully what would happen if the Merovingians or their supporters learned they had designs on the throne.

"We drink freely of this cup." Egar held up the chalice. "If insincere in our intent to remain silent of this secret, may the potion we swallow cause that which brings life to spew forth in a fountain. Better to die now than reveal this family's awesome destiny."

Egar gazed into the liquid within the spider-carved chalice. He emptied his mind of all thought except the oath to which he was binding himself. Raising the cup to his lips, he swallowed a mouthful of the bitter-tasting concoction. Its thickness and taste made him gag slightly, convulsing his body as he made a soft retching sound.

Seeing Egar's reaction to the potion, each person in turn paused to think, then steel himself, before following his lead.

"You need not do this," said Egar to Pepin, "if, to save your soul, you feel compelled to confess this to your priest. I would not stand between you and your God."

"This has nothing to do with the priests," said Pepin. "Hand me the chalice. I will drink my share."

"May our tongues be cut from our bodies—" Egar took up the gleaming knife, "—should word of our secret be spoken to any except those descended from Pepin's loins."

Holding the knife, Egar closed his eyes and touched the tip of his tongue to its cutting edge. Immediately blood spurt in a thin red stream. Bending over the saucer, he caught the precious fluid.

Bega gave out an involuntary moan and seemed ready to faint. Itta caught her, holding her until she had regained control. One after the other, each of them added their blood to that on the saucer.

Egar held the saucer aloft reverently in both hands. "We vow to support one another. And to repeat this service when any of Pepin's seed shall come of age, from this night forth until the great king takes his crown."

So saying, Egar touched his throbbing tongue to the combined blood on the saucer. At once the pain disappeared and the cut was miraculously healed. Each person smiled in wonder and relief as they followed his actions.

"We have done all in our power," Egar said quietly. "The future is in the hands of the gods."

Chapter Thirty-Seven

Peace settled over Pepin's chamber as each of his family came to terms with the weight of their foreknowledge.

Wearily, Pepin opened his eyes, beckoning to Egar. His voice was so weak Egar had to lean his ear near Pepin's mouth to make out what he said.

"Take my ring."

"That should be Grimwald's, surely," objected Egar.

"Grimwald has what he needs. And if... it is to be his, you will give it to him. I want... you to keep it safe... for the great king. Give it to him from my hand, to yours, to his."

Egar held the proffered hand with its ring tenderly in his own, not knowing how to respond.

"When you write the story..." Pepin began.

"But, I am not going to write it," Egar protested. "The monks are the historians. I will merely relate it to them."

Pepin wearily raised his hand to stop Egar. "No. You must write it. They will not... do not know..."

Egar could see Pepin's strength was about gone. "I will see it gets written," he reassured the dying man.

"You must... do it yourself..." Pepin licked his dry lips and closed his eyes. "Promise me."

"You have my word. I... I will scribe it myself."

Wearily, Pepin nodded his head. "Take the ring."

Egar gently slipped the ring off Pepin's finger. With a sigh, he put it on his own. He felt the burden not only of the massive piece of jewelry but the promise it signified. In accepting it, a tangible symbol of the prophecy, Egar acknowledged his destiny as guardian of the future until he could hand it to him who would rule in greatness.

He gripped Grimwald's arm in compassion. Egar sensed no animosity there, only Grimwald's determination to earn for himself the right to wear the ring if he could.

He turned once more to gaze at Pepin. "Farewell, my friend. God speed you to the light."

For several moments no one spoke. Pepin shuddered. Rasped. Then breathed no more.

Itta let out the long wailing cry of an injured animal. Feeling his own throat tighten, Egar watched the family form a tight knot. There seemed no room for him within the group. He had been absent from their lives too long.

Gently he touched Itta's hand in condolence, receiving an infinitely sad smile in return. Only Bega broke with the closed family circle to give Egar a sisterly embrace. A moment later he turned and left Pepin's room, his eyes filled with tears.

Carefully weaving his way through the sleeping forms in the darkened hall, Egar finally pushed open the wooden door to the bailey. Rain had fallen during the night. The scent of wet earth and water-soaked wood pricked his nose. Weary, Egar sank to a nearby log.

Arriving that afternoon, tired from the journey, he had learned of Pepin's imminent death. Since then his emotions had been buffeted like a small round boat on a storm-tossed sea.

And now, Pepin was gone.

Egar's chest felt as though a heavy weight had pressed out all breath. His throat ached with the lump lodged there. At last the tears fell unchecked. Burying his head in his hands, he sobbed, knowing he was alone and no one could hear. He cried for himself, for the loss of yet one more friend whom he had come to love.

As the wracking shudders grew less, he thought forlornly of his life stretching endless before him. He would have to find vellum, ink and quills. It would take years to get the words right.

At this moment he wanted nothing so much as to take his belongings and return with Dione to the serenity of their cave. He longed for the simple life amid their friends.

Dione! Could he expect her to stay while he spent every daylight hour writing? No. She belonged where she could roam the out-of-doors in freedom and safety.

Just then he felt her hand upon his shoulder.

"Is... is it over for Pepin, then?" she whispered.

Egar nodded, not trusting his voice. She wrapped him in her arms. Her sympathy brought a return of the painful tightening to Egar's throat. It was hard to swallow the hot tears he would not shed in her presence.

The sky to the east had lightened to iridescence, the walls and trees forming a black silhouette. The two of them stood together in silence for several moments. Then arm in arm, they walked to the barred palisade gate.

"Be ye Egar the Sorcerer?" asked the guard.

"Yes."

"Be Pepin...?"

The pain once again assailed Egar, threatening to erupt. "Yes." It was a mere whisper.

Without further word the guard opened the gate. Egar and Dione walked out without looking back.

They did not stop until they reached the giant oak that had been Egar's refuge many years past when he had, from time to time, escaped Dagobert's court for the solitude of the forest. The huge trunk and exposed roots of the old tree shielded him like a mother's arms. Dione curled up at his feet. Neither of them spoke while the dawn sun silently bathed the topmost branches of the forest in liquid gold.

At last Egar looked up. Dione's eye was attracted by the heavy gold ring on his finger, fashioned in the shape of a shield with a rounded, five-pointed design in the center.

"Pepin's ring?" she asked.

Egar nodded and told her of Pepin's last request.

"He was likely right, you know," she said when he finished. "You should write it in a monastery scriptorium."

"I doubt a monastery would allow a non-believer to enter," Egar said. "They would never give me writing materials. Nor guard the finished book."

"Scriptoria are set aside for the copying and writing of all knowledge, both sacred and profane," offered Dione. "They will respect your writing because it is part of the history of this kingdom and because Pepin gave his ring to ensure it. You must commence immediately while your knowledge of Pepin is still clear. Writing will ease the pain of his death."

"But the cathedral here in Metz has no scriptorium. Where should I go?" Egar thought for a while and then brightening asked, "Would you go with me to Paris? The monastery on the Left Bank has a scriptorium where I could write. I might go if you would go with me."

Dione tilted her head and sat as if waiting for some direction from the gods. At last she smiled. "I would *love* to explore Paris."

Chapter Thirty-Eight

They found a room at an inn on the île de la Cité. Egar intended to earn their keep by singing together in the evenings.

Next morning he walked to the Abbey of St. Germain-des-Prés to make arrangements to go there during daylight hours to write "Pepin's Song", as he now thought of it.

Egar returned from that audience shortly after noon in a foul mood. "Pack up our things, we are leaving," he ordered Dione as he entered their small room.

"What did they say to you?"

"I wish not to discuss it. I will write of Pepin in our cave on whatever scraps of vellum we can afford to buy." Egar grabbed a bag and began stuffing clothes into it.

"What *did* they say?" Dione put her hands on his chest, forcing him to stop his frantic activity and sit. She knelt at his feet, peering into his face.

At last he sighed and said, "The priests said we are living in sin because we have not been married by their Christian God."

"Merely that?" Dione laughed. "Who gives a fig what they think?"

"There is more. They will not allow me writing materials nor permit me into the scriptorium as long as we live together."

He sighed again. "If I leave you, they will allow me to dwell with the lay brothers and provide me with writing materials and food. They will not admit me any other way."

Egar paused, thinking of the enormity of their demands. "It will take a goodly time to write and once I enter the monastery, I may not withdraw until I am finished. Once I depart those walls, I may not re-enter. It is too great a price to pay. I will not do it. We are leaving Paris, now, this very day." Egar stood once more and began pacing the small room.

"Wait. Vellum is dear. We could never earn enough to pay for it. And what about your promise to Pepin? Any promise is a vow but one made on a death-bed is doubly binding. You may not walk away from it."

"Our love is just as binding," Egar argued.

"We will love each other forever." Dione touched her heart. "But we always knew we were to remain together only at the pleasure of the gods. Although it causes pain, this may be their will as well."

Egar threw down the bag. "That cannot be! I will not accept it!"

"Be true to your destiny. To turn your back on that would be to rob your life of meaning." Dione rose to face Egar, gazing into his eyes with a searching look. "How would you have your life judged?"

Words from long ago sounded in his ears. His master's voice. *"It is your destiny after all. Only you can decide to what extent you will allow it to be your guide."* And then, *"Truly followed, your life will change the course of Frankish history."*

"But what would happen to you?"

"The gods watch over me," Dione said simply.

"Where would you go?" Egar paused then said slowly, "Return to Itta. She will be lonely now and pleased with your company."

"Perhaps. Though I think she will enter a religious life. Well-born widows generally do. But," Dione smiled, some of her normal cheerfulness returning, "I will have much to see and do. In time, I might go to Bega and live with them in Landen. She might welcome me."

"I have known since the first we would be separated before I could wish it," said Egar. "But I always thought you would precipitate the parting, never me."

"It is our fate for having been chosen by the gods," said Dione gently.

"You must find a good man and allow yourself to love and be loved." Egar stood and took her hands in his. "Your life must not stretch ahead of you, empty and forbidding."

Dione looked up at him, tears shimmering in her eyes. "I have been loved by a sorcerer. What more could any life offer?"

"Then go to Bega. When I finish the writing, if the gods grant it, I will come to you in Landen." Egar felt the first faint stirring of hope rising in his chest. "Knowing you wait for me will speed me at my task."

Egar wrapped Dione in his arms and kissed her as if to imprint his love indelibly on her lips. She clung to him, allowing herself to be held, their bodies becoming one entity for a few precious moments. Then she broke away.

"When must you return?" she asked.

"Before vespers this very day."

"What may you take with you?"

"My clothes, my harp, and the love for you that will dwell in my heart for as long as it shall beat."

Silently they finished piling his clothes into the bag. They loaded it and his harp on Smoke and walked, arm in arm, down the cobblestone streets of Paris. She would keep Smoke as her own. The noise and crush of people and animals did not intrude on their world. Their awareness extended only as far as each other.

They crossed the bridge. Salty tears sprang to Egar's eyes despite his attempts to blink them away.

With feet as heavy as their hearts, they climbed the Montagne Sainte Geneviéve. Too soon they reached the gate in the wall.

Dione turned to him. "I know I cannot see the scriptorium or the room where you will sleep, but let me go with you into the cathedral. I need a picture in my mind of what it looks like where you are."

"I will *not* enter the cathedral to worship their God!"

"You will continue to worship the gods that guide your life wherever you find them. Why not in the quiet of this holy place? Are they so different from the Christian God that they cannot be found side by side? And when you worship, you will know I am thinking of you and wishing you well."

Dione kissed him gently. Entering the door they stood in awed silence. Dusky shadows stretched ahead of them broken by shafts of sunlight streaming slant-wise through the narrow wind openings. Candles twinkled like fallen stars on the altar far away at the other end.

Egar stood there, feeling very small, as the tranquility of the place drove away the rebellion inside him. In its place descended the peace of acceptance. He did not know how long he stood there. Was not aware of Dione slipping away. The peacefulness was broken by the sound of the door banging shut.

The sound reverberated through the cathedral, echoing as it rolled along the stone floor, against stone walls, bounced from the stone ceiling. He wondered if it would never cease. Would he hear it ringing in his head until he died?

At last the awful thunder was replaced by the sound of Dione's musical laugh. *I have been loved by a sorcerer. What more could any life offer?* And I have been loved by Dione, he thought.

Smiling sadly, he walked out of the cathedral to where Smoke had been tied. The animal was gone, carrying his love on its sturdy back. Egar picked up his bag and harp and rang the bell. A brother opened the gate.

With a bitter-sweet mixture of sorrow and expectation, Egar took the fateful steps that would carry him inside this community closed to the outside world.

The beginning had come to an end. He would live as one of the brothers, accepting as his own the pallet which would be his bed, the trencher from which he would eat with them in silence, and the desk which would be his for as long as it took him to write "Pepin's Song".

What would happen when once this task was done until the coming of the great king he could only guess. But he found the devastating pain of Pepin's death and his separation from Dione beginning to ease.

He strode toward the dormitory building, looking forward to what next the gods had in store for him. He felt a surge of excitement envelope him, as though Dione had wrapped him in the benediction of her loving arms.

Afterword

The coming of the great king took far longer than Egar could have guessed. Time and again the magician returned to the scriptorium in Paris to write additional chapters in the history book of the Franks.

After Pepin the Vain's death, Grimwald served as mayor of the palace for King Sigibert III. When Sigibert died, Grimwald sent Sigibert's son, eight-year-old Dagobert II, to Ireland where he was consecrated a monk. Seeking the promised crown, Grimwald claimed Dagobert had died, and furthermore that Sigibert had adopted his own son, Childebert.

Grimwald persuaded his partisans to elevate Childebert on his shield as King of Austrasia. This rash act incurred the jealous opposition of magnates from Neustria and Burgundy who were not about to accept as king, a youth who was not of royal Merovingian blood. Childebert reigned as king for only a few days. Disaffected Austrasians in league with the Neustrians, seized him and his father and transported them to the court of Clovis II in Burgundy. Clovis threw both Grimwald and Childebert into prison. They were bound with chains, tortured, and finally killed.

Clovis II, who had been made king of Burgundy by Dagobert when he was five years old, assumed actual rule at age seven. He grew up to be a bestial libertine. According to the history books, "He had every kind of filthy habit. He was a seducer and a debaser of women, a glutton and a drunk. His mind became affected."

Nanthild, his mother, chose an efficient and relatively just mayor of the palace and ruled with him until Clovis became titular king.

Clovis II married Balthild, an Anglo-Saxon slave girl who grew into a rational and attractive woman. Balthild ruled as regent in her husband's periods of insanity, along with a good mayor of the palace. Together these two intelligent people maintained peace for the eighteen years of Mad King Clovis II's reign.

When Clovis II died, Balthild, who had prohibited the sale of Christian slaves and herself purchased freedom for many of them, turned to the religious life. She founded the double monastery of Chelles. The Merovingian rule had degenerated into "do nothing kings" *les rois fainéants*.

Meanwhile, with Grimwald's death, Pepin's family lost the hereditery right to rule as mayors of the palace. Leaderless, the country was paralyzed. Some self-serving noblemen tried to consolidate power by backing figurehead Merovingian children. Others tried to grab the power behind the throne for themselves.

Pepin de Gros (Fat Pepin), son of Bega and Ansegisel stepped into the breach, first as duke of Austrasia and later as mayor of the palace. Inch by inch, estate by estate, he consolidated the country once more. Although he outlived his two legitimate sons, he did have a bastard son named Charles.

However, the story of "Pepin's Bastard" is another book.■

Bibliography

Asimov, Isaac, *The Dark Ages*, Houghton Mifflin Co.,
   Boston, 1968.
Ault, Warren O., *Europe in the Middle Ages*, D.C.
   Heath & Co., Boston, 1932.
Brooks, Polly Schoyer & Nancy Zinsser Walworth, *The
   World of Walls, The Middle Ages in Western
   Europe*, J.B. Lippincott Co., Philadelphia & New
   York, 1966.
Bullough, Donald A., *The Age of Charlemagne*,
   Putnam, New York, 1966.
Cairns, Conrad, *Medieval Castles*, Lerner Publications
   Co., Minneapolis in cooperation with Cambridge
   University Press, 1989.
Crombie, A.C., *Medieval & Early Modern Science, Vol.
   1*, Garden City: Doubleday & Co., 1952.
Easton, Stewart Copinger, *Era of Charlemagne;
   Frankish State & Society*, Van Nostrand, Princeton,
   New Jersey, 1961.

Eco, Umberto, *The Name of the Rose*, Harcourt Brace Javanovich, San Diego, 1983.

Einhard, *The Life of Charlemagne*, Ann Arbor: University of Michigan.

Funck-Bretans, Frank, translated by E.F. Buckley, *The Earliest Times*, G.P. Putnam's Sons, 1927.

Gergerding, Richard A., *The Rise of the Carolingians and the Liber Historiae Francorum*, Clarendon Press, Oxford, 1987.

Halphen, Louis, *Charlemagne and the Carolingian Empire*, North Holland Pub. Co., Amsterdam, New York, 1977.

Hartman, Gertrude, *Medieval Days and Ways*, The Macmillan Co., New York, 1958.

Hassall, Arthur, *France Medieval and Modern*, Oxford at the Clarendon Press, 1919.

Hyde, M.P. *The Singing Sward*, Little, 1930.

James, Edward, *The Franks*, B.Blackwell, Oxford, U.K., N.Y., 1988.

Kamrodd, Manuel, *Charlemagne*, Julian Messner Inc., New York, 1964.

Lasko, Peter, *Kingdom of the Franks*, McFraw-Hill, New York, 1971.

Linnell, Gertrude, *Behind the Battlements*, McMillan, 1931.

Magoon, Marian, *Little Dusty Foot*, Longmans, 1948.

Magoon, Marion, *The Emperor's Nephew*, Farrar & Rinehart, Inc., New York.

Mills, Dorothy, *The Middle Ages*, G.P. Putnam's Sons, 1935.

Pirenne, Henri, *Economic and Social History of Medieval Europe*, Harcourt, Brace & Co., New York, 1956.

Power, Eileen, *Medieval People*, Barnes & Noble Inc. University Paperbacks, New York, 1963.

Pyle, Kenneth Daingerfield, *The Daingerfield Family Tree*, Unpublished, 1938.

Riché, Pierre, translated by JoAnn McNamara, *Daily Life in the World of Charlemagne,* University of Pennsylvania Press, 1978.

Rutherfurd, Edward, *Sarum,* Ivy Books, Ballantine Books, Pub., 1987.

Scherman, Katherine, *The Birth of France, Warriors, Bishops and Long-Haired Kings,* Random House, New York, 1987.

Simons, Gerald, *Barbarian Europe,* Time-Life Books (Great Ages of Man Series), 1968.

Sobol, Donald J. Illus. Lili Rethi, *The First Book of Medieval Man,* Franklin Watts, Inc., 575 Lexington Avenue, New York, 1924.

Tours, Gregory of, *Historia Francorum,* (translated), Penguin, Harmondsworth, Baltimore, 1974.

van Dyke, Paul, *The Story of France from Julieus Caesar to Napoleon III,* Charles Scribner's Sons, New York, London, 1929.

Wallace-Hadrill, J.M., *The Long-Haired Kings,* Barnes & Noble, Inc. New York, 1962.

Winston, Richard, *Charlemange, From the Hammer to the Cross,* The Bobbs-Merrill Co., Indianapolis, 1954.

Destiny's Godchild
by Diana M. Johnson

Order copies of ***Destiny's Godchild*** now. Personally autographed copies available on request. Order several, they make unique gifts.

___(Quantity) Destiny's Godchild   ISBN 0-9661504-0-6 $12.00

Autograph copy to: _____
                         (please print clearly)

Additional copies to: _____

_____

Send to:
         Name_____

         Address_____

         City_____State____Zip_____

Enclose $12.00 per book ordered above _ _ _ _ _ _____
<u>plus</u>
Postage and handling _ _ _ _ _ _ _ _   _   _____
($4 for the first book and $1 for each additional book.)

Applicable California sales tax _ _ _ _ _ _ _   _____

                Total _ _ _ _ _ _ _ _ _ _____

Send check or money order (no cash or CODs) to:
Superior Book Publishing Company, PO Box 8312,
Van Nuys, CA 91409.
Prices subject to change without notice.
Valid in the U.S. only.